I0778979

THE FATES

COVEN: BOOK 14

DAVID NETH

DN Publishing

The Fates

Coven, Book 14

Copyright © 2025 by David Neth

Batavia, NY

www.DavidNethBooks.com

ISBN: 978-1-963602-30-2
First Edition

Subscribe to the author's newsletter for updates and exclusive content:
DavidNethBooks.com/Newsletter

Follow the author at:
www.facebook.com/DavidNethBooks
www.instagram.com/dnpublishing

Also by David Neth

Lost By Magic
Lost By Magic
Lucky By Magic
Lured By Magic

Coven
Harpy
Siren
Valkyrie
Shapeshifter
Sorcerer
Witch (Short Story)
Enchantress
Oracle
Trickster
Poltergeist
Hex (Short Story)
Witch Hunter
Demon (Short Story)
Necromancer
Psychic (Short Story)
Incubus
Spirit (Short Story)
Human
Krampus (Short Story)
The Fates

Under the Moon
The Full Moon
The Harvest Moon
The Blood Moon
The Crescent Moon
The Blue Moon

The Art of Magic

Under the Moon: Villains
Toxanna (Short Story)
The Queen (Short Story)
The Dark Knight (Short Story)

Fuse
Origin
Omertá
Oblivion

Heat
Black Magnet
Dust Storm
The Gatekeeper

Standalone
All I Ever Wanted

CHAPTER 1

- JANUARY 1991 -

Samantha and Kathy sprinted through the night. The winter wind whipped around them, but they paid it no mind. They charged on over the city roads covered with slush from the previous day's snow.

The trouble was, they didn't know where exactly they were running to. Kathy's power had recently grown. Now, instead of her time specialty allowing her to only momentarily freeze people in time, her powers allowed her to witness moments in a future time, right in her mind. Premonitions. Psychic visions. Whatever it was called, she could, in a sense, see the future.

And what she saw terrified her.

"What did it look like in the vision?" Samantha's head was craned to the left as she looked down driveways along W 21st

Street. Kathy, meanwhile, inspected the houses to the right.

"It was just a skinny driveway," Kathy said. "A garage at the back of it. A small yard beside it. Just like all of these—"

A man's screams cut her off. Somewhere down toward the end of the block. Near Chestnut Street.

The girls sped up to reach it faster, but the cries died off.

"Where did it come from?" Kathy stopped and looked around.

"This way." Samantha led her sister to a house that seemed to be very well-kept. The biggest flaws were some worn siding and cracked sidewalks in front. Even the car parked in the driveway looked to be newer. Maybe an '88 or '89.

At the back of the driveway, though, they saw two men who appeared to be kissing. Upon closer inspection, they saw that they weren't actually kissing. Instead, the one man was biting the other.

"A vampire?" Samantha asked.

"Just like I saw." Kathy raced up. "Hey! Leave him alone!"

The man who had been bitten fell to the ground. His neck dripped with blood. The skin around it looked inflamed and angry.

Not half as angry as the other man, who remained standing. The one whose face looked as white as a ghost and who had blood dripping around his mouth. The one who wore sharp clothing, all in black. An odd sight for the setting.

"No!" Samantha called. "You killed him!"

"I improved him," the pale man said. "Perhaps you'd like to be next?" He lunged at them and the sisters jumped back. He laughed at their fear.

Kathy pulled a wooden stake from her jacket pocket and passed it to Samantha. "Here! I pulled it from the garage before we left."

The older sister grumbled as she took the small weapon. Her eyes remained on the vampire in front of them. She had never battled with one before and she didn't like the idea of having to get so close to him in order to stop him.

Kathy pulled a second stake from her pocket and the sisters spread out, splitting the vampire's focus.

As the three of them squared off, the vampire took several lunges at the witches to scare them, but never made contact. Kathy knew that if he wanted to, he could strike them down faster than either of them could. What they needed was a distraction. A way to split the vampire's focus even further. Like—

"Kathy! The car!" Samantha noticed that the car in the driveway had a combination lock on the door handle. Something equipped with that level of safety likely had an alarm as well.

Kathy looked to her sister, then down to the car. In one quick jab, she slammed the tip of the stake into the hood of the car. Instantly, the alarm sounded and the headlights began flashing.

THE FATES

The vampire shielded his eyes as the lights on the car began to flash. Meanwhile, behind him, his latest victim began to rise to his feet. His skin had turned a ghostly shade of white, just like his attacker's. What was more, the bite mark on his neck had faded completely, leaving only dried blood in its place.

"Uh…" Samantha hesitated as she suddenly realized that there were *two* vampires to contend with now.

The first vampire stepped back next to the second and smirked at the witches. "You're too late. He's now officially one of us. You're too late."

Kathy put up her hands to freeze them, but the first vampire hissed at them and she jumped. When she turned to try again, they were gone.

"Well, that was unexpected," Samantha said.

"And unfortunate," Kathy said. "We lost an innocent man and created a monster."

Samantha looked around. "Yeah, and we need to get out of here before one of the neighbors calls the cops about the noise from this car and then *we're* being investigated for his disappearance."

While neither of them liked the fact that they had lost someone they were meant to protect, their only choice left was to protect themselves. So off they ran.

CHAPTER 2

I promised you I'd make it up to you." Samantha presented her husband with a cup of coffee as he sat in the living room.

Josh was tucked in close next to his dad, his eyes glued on the TV.

Steven laughed and reached for the cup. "Not quite the romantic evening I was expecting, but I guess I'll take it."

Their two-year anniversary dinner had been interrupted by the urgency of Kathy's vision the night before. And the fact that they hadn't even been able to save the man was just more salt in the wound.

"Honey, it's okay." He set the mug down on the end table, then reached for his his wife's hand and pulled her into his lap.

"Mom, go 'way!"

"That's not nice," Steven scolded in a soft tone. "We don't say that."

Josh had already moved on, reverting to his zombie-like state as he watched the cartoons dance across the television screen.

Samantha didn't like how much they let Josh watch TV, but sometimes it was the only way to get things done around the house. And other than in the mornings on the weekends and every evening, he didn't watch nearly as much as some other kids. Then again, what Kathy let him do while they were at work was out of Samantha's control.

"I was a little annoyed last night, yes," Steven went on.

She scoffed. "More than a little…"

"But I got over it," he said. "After I put Josh to bed, it was nice to have the house to myself for a change. I got to watch a little TV of my own. Have my own snack."

She raised her eyebrows. "So you're saying you don't want a makeup for last night?"

He smirked. "I didn't say *that*. In fact, I think you owe me."

Samantha feigned ignorance. "Doesn't the coffee cover it?"

"Oh, not even close!"

She laughed and leaned in to kiss him.

"Have your sister watch Josh tonight," he said. "We can book a hotel room."

Another burst of laughter. "Okay. Let's not get wild here."

He pulled her even closer. Not that there was any way that was possible. She was already sitting in his lap. "I just want to be alone with you."

"And I want the same thing," she said. "And we will. Tonight. We'll go to dinner, then come back here after Josh has gone to bed. Maybe Kathy will be cozy down here in the living room so you and I can get cozy upstairs—"

She stopped and pulled away from her husband. "Steven?"

He wasn't moving. Wasn't reacting to anything she was saying, like he had been moments before.

Then she realized that the TV wasn't playing anything anymore either. She craned around and saw that it was frozen.

"Kathy!" she called up the stairs. Samantha tried to extract herself from her husband's grip, which had been a loving embrace only moments ago but now felt like a prison. "Kathy! Did you freeze us?"

Seconds later, her younger sister raced down the stairs. "Sam! What's going on? Everything outside has stopped! I was watching the snow fall and then—hey, what happened to Steven?" Kathy scrunched her eyebrows together when she saw that he was sitting with his arms in the same position they had been when they were wrapped around his wife.

"You mean *you* didn't do this?"

"My power has grown, sure, but not that much!" Kathy said. "I was actually just upstairs reading about premonitions and I think my power is growing in a whole different way than all of this."

"Then who did this?" Samantha was equally confused as her sister.

"Well, I'll tell you, Clo, I could see that coming a mile away!" an old woman said from the dining room. "He's had his eye on her since they were kids!"

"But she loved Greg," another lady's voice said. "They were engaged! I thought the two of them had what it takes!"

A third lady scoffed. "Oh, please, Atro. Nothing beats out your first true love. Nobody else compares!"

The sisters eyed each other, then stepped around the corner into the dining room. Three old women sat at the end of the table. Each of them had knitting needles in their hands, working away at different parts of the large tapestry that lay across the dining room table, extending off the end of it and spilling onto the floor on the opposite side. The tapestry had a unique and beautiful design, although there were many imperfections. Knots and lines out of place from the patterns, even though the whole of it still was something to marvel.

"Excuse me?" Samantha asked, suddenly feeling as though she needed to be polite even though these women had invaded *her* house. "Who are you?"

The woman sitting in the middle turned around and looked at them, then held her hand to her chest as she laughed. "Oh! Honey, you scared me!"

"You have to be careful, Clo, or we'd have to find someone else to finish up Taylor Miller's stitch work," the woman to her left said.

"We might as well," the third one said. "Look how she's gone and messed it all up. Clo, that stitching is horrendous!"

"Me? It's not *my* fault!"

Kathy cleared her throat. "Who the hell are you people?"

"Oh, my apologies!" the lady on the left said. "My name is Lachesis, but the girls here call me Lakie for short. Then there's Clotho, or Clo, and over there is Atropos, but we just call her Atro." She indicated with a head nod who she was talking about.

"Why are you here?" Samantha asked.

"Well, we're the Fates," Lakie said.

"We typically don't allow ourselves to be seen," Atro cut in, all the while keeping her eyes on her stitching.

"But we thought this was especially necessary," Clo added.

"You see," Lakie picked up, "you've failed in your duties as witches."

Kathy raised her eyebrows. "Excuse me?"

"Is this about last night?" Samantha asked. "We did the best we could!"

"Ah!" Atro raised a finger, then resumed her needlework. "But your best was not enough."

"You can't blame us for that!" Samantha said. "We tried. We failed. Evil spread. Someone's life is essentially over. Don't you think we already feel terrible about all of that?"

"We can't save *every* person," Kathy added. "As hard as we try to."

"But you see, from that terrible *mistake*, you have significantly altered the course of time," Clo said.

"Altered the fates of so many others," Lakie said.

Samantha tucked her hair behind her ears, then put her hands on her hips. "What are you talking about? Nobody else was there last night."

"We're not talking about the past," Atro said. "We're talking about the future."

"We're not responsible for the future!" Kathy blurted.

"Ah, but in fact, you are." Clo waved her needle in the direction of the witches. "With every life you save, you preserve the future. And with every life lost…"

"Just take a look at the tapestry." Lakie pointed out the line of stitching she was working on. Although the sisters knew nothing about how knitting and crocheting worked, they both could see that the line of stitching had gone severely off-course from the rest of the design.

"Oh, yes, that's terrible, Lakie," Atro said.

She shrugged. "It was the best I could do with what I was given!"

"Will someone explain to us what's going on?" Samantha demanded.

"In terms that we can understand," Kathy added.

"This is the tapestry of time," Atro explained.

"Collectively, as the Fates, we stitch it together based on the actions of those in the world," Lakie added.

"Each person's actions affect someone else's life in one or another," Clo said. "Like our lives, the tapestry is tightly woven together."

"But it's not without mistakes," Lakie said.

"Look at this line here." Clo pointed to a knot in the tapestry. "This was the moment you two failed to save Stockley from Aldric's bite."

"Stockley? Aldric?" Kathy asked. "Were those the names of the men last night?"

"The *vampires*," Lakie corrected.

"The undead," Clo added.

"The ones who wish to defy the work we do," Atro finished.

"In the future, those two vampires have gone on to gain too much power," Lakie said.

"Witches, wizards, and even good-hearted vampires cannot stop them," Clo said.

"And the rest of humanity has had to suffer from their reign," Atro said.

"In the future, we, as the Fates, have no influence over anyone's choices," Lakie explained. "The vampires are in *complete* control."

"And that will lead to the end of our tapestry," Clo explained. "Something we've been creating since the dawn of humanity."

The Fates

Kathy crossed her arms, feeling the guilt of their misstep hit her hard. "So you came here just to tell us we screwed up and that, because of us, humanity is going to die?"

All three women looked at each other, then burst out laughing.

"No!" Clo blurted.

"You two don't wield that kind of power!" Lakie said, still chuckling.

"We came here to ask for your help!" Atro clarified.

"And you thought you'd start off by insulting us?" Kathy asked.

Lakie rolled her eyes and shook her head. "Oh, please! The *dramatics* of these witches! No, we were simply alerting you to the problem!"

"And so what kind of help were you hoping to get out of us?" Samantha asked.

"We want to offer something we've never done before," Atro said.

"We will unravel part of our tapestry so that the two of you can unknot out tapestry and restore order," Lakie explained.

"In a sense, we will be turning back time to allow you to fix what you failed to do before," Clo said.

There was a significant silence that followed the Fates' proposition. Samantha and Kathy both turned to each other. Even without Samantha's telepathic abilities, they knew what the other was thinking.

"And you expect us to agree to that?" Samantha asked.

"You have to!" Atro said, all laughter from her face gone.

"We don't *have to* do anything," Kathy said. "Look, we're sorry that you're disappointed in us—we're also sorry we weren't able to save that man last night—but *you* try doing our job for a day and see if you have a perfect streak!"

"And we're not going to risk going back in time," Samantha said. "There are too many variables. Even with your foresight as the Fates."

"Yeah, how do we know that you even have that kind of power?" Kathy added. "How do we know you're not going to slip up and send us back fifteen years and we'll have to relive a chunk of our lives and hope that everything turns out the same?"

"That's a lot of trust you're asking of us, all for one single vampire that we let be created."

Lakie rose from her seat. "A vampire that will help lead to the end of humanity as we know it! A vampire that will help turn all of civilization into mindless vampiric *zombies* if they don't follow willingly."

"These vampires will be out of our control!" Atro said. "Without you correcting your mistake, we have no ability to influence how these circumstances will play out."

"Sounds like a problem for you," Kathy said. "Not us."

"Wait." Clo remained calm. Her knitting needles no longer moving. "I have a proposition for you girls, seeing as though you have your…hesitations."

THE FATES

Samantha put her hands on her hips. "And that would be…?"

"What if we sent you *forward* in time, so you can witness the destruction yourselves?"

The two other Fates gasped.

"But that would require starting a new tapestry from scratch!" Lakie said.

"We've never done that before!" Atro added.

"For this, I'm willing to take the time," Clo said. "And with the present paused—and possibly remade—it's work we'd have to do anyway." Her eyes darted to the sisters. "You'd be able to see firsthand how bad this world is that we're trying to avoid. That way, you'll have no choice but to agree to help us stop it."

Samantha and Kathy both studied her, intrigued by the proposition, but fearful for what it might entail.

"So…what do you say?" Clo asked.

"Can we talk about this privately?" Kathy asked.

"Go ahead." Clo gestured for them to go.

Samantha and Kathy stepped into the living room, where Steven and Josh were still frozen on the couch. Moments later, they heard the giggling and cackling of laughter from the Fates as they resumed their gossip.

"I'm not sure about this," Samantha said in a hushed tone to her sister. "It seems too risky."

Kathy shrugged. "I don't know. I think it might be kind of

fun to see our future selves. I mean, when are we ever going to get the chance to again?"

"But what if we can't get back?"

"The Fates are sending us, I don't think we'll have a problem getting back. Besides, it's the future, not the past. So we won't even need to be careful about changing anything because when we come back to the present, everything we do in the future will be reset."

"Will it, though?" Samantha gestured toward the dining room. "With the Fates out there, everything is pre-destined, isn't it?"

Kathy shook her head. "No, they said it doesn't work like that. We still have free will. The future is made up of limitless possibilities. Fate only outlines those possibilities based on our choices made by our free will."

Samantha crossed her arms and looked at her sister. "When did you become an expert on this?"

"About five minutes ago when they explained how it works." She eyed her sister. "You don't think we can trust them."

"I didn't say that."

"But it's true."

"Okay." Samantha shrugged. "So I'm not sure we should. Is that so bad?"

"No. It's natural to be cautious—especially with our history. But they're the *Fates*, Sam! If we can't trust them, who can we trust? Besides, nothing ever happens in life without a little trust."

Samantha rolled her eyes. "All right, enough with the pop psychology tidbits. I'm just not sure I want to see that future they're talking about if it's so bad."

"So then we let them send us back in time to yesterday, and we can stop the vampires and avoid all of this."

Samantha breathed out a sigh, still unsure. "I just…I don't know how one simple vampire could be so dire."

Kathy looked down at her nails. "Well, the only way we're going to know that is by having the Fates send us into the future. And we can have some fun with it, too. See Josh all grown up—and the new baby."

Samantha's hand went to her belly. Her second pregnancy hadn't started showing yet, but the signs were there. Hormonal shifts. Cravings. Other changes to her body.

What a gift it would be to glimpse her children in the future. Nobody, as far as she knew, had ever had the chance before.

"Okay, think of it this way," Kathy went on. "Even if it turns out that we *can't* trust the Fates and we're suddenly stuck in this terrible future, all we need to do is track down your kids and our future selves and have them help us get back to this time. After all, each generation of magic is stronger than the next. Hopefully time travel is right on the cusp of magic."

Samantha sighed and nodded. "I mean, that does alleviate my fears a little bit."

"Then let's go give them our answer." Kathy led them back to the living room, where the three Fates were working away, giggling and joking and talking as if they hadn't just given the sisters such a monumental offer.

"So?" Clo asked. "What have you decided?"

"We'll take your offer to glimpse the future," Kathy said.

Atro smiled. "We knew you'd make the right choice."

"Just one question," Samantha cut in.

"Of course!" Clo said cheerfully.

"This won't affect our present lives at all?"

Atro shook her head. "Not at all. You will be traveling to a version of the future that we predict based on your current actions. Whatever happens in the future stays in the future."

"Almost like Vegas," Lakie said with a giggle. "So, are you ready?"

"Now?" Samantha blurted. "We're going *now*? Don't we get to say goodbye to our family?"

"Why?" Clo asked. "Sure, *you* will be leaving for a while, but when you come back you'll come right back to this moment. Steven and Josh—and the rest of the world, for that matter—will be unaware that time had frozen at all."

"We'll simply hit pause on reality and are going to pluck you into a different one for a little while before dropping you back in this one and letting it play again," Atro explained.

Kathy looked over and saw that her sister was starting to get cold feet, so she plunged on with what they had already decided.

THE FATES

"Okay. So what do we need to…"

Her words trailed off as an intense light came over them. And then they were gone.

CHAPTER 3

"Do?" Kathy finished slowly as the wave of light passed. She looked around the house—her house—and didn't initially notice anything different.

But after a few seconds, all the differences started rolling in, coming at her like sensory overload.

First off, the Fates were no longer sitting at the dining room table.

Second, the temperature was now much warmer—almost sticky. One quick glance outside told her that it was now summer time. A far cry from the wintry mid-January conditions that they were in moments before.

She picked up on little things next. For one, the flowers on the dining room table were different. The pictures on the walls, many of which of people she didn't quite recognize. Even the rug underneath the dining room table wasn't the same as it had been in Kathy's time.

"Are you okay?" Samantha asked, breaking into Kathy's thoughts.

"Yeah. Just taking it all in."

"I know. It's weird. It's the same but…not." Samantha stepped into the living room, which was empty of people.

"What is it?" Kathy joined her and noticed that the furniture had changed, as did the books on the shelves.

"Steven and Josh are gone."

"Well, yeah. It's the future."

"But then…where are they? Where am I? My future self, that is. Or did we take the place of our future selves?"

Kathy stepped toward the front door and glanced in the mirror that hung beside the coat rack. Glad to know at least some things were the same. Like, for instance, her face.

"Well, I don't look any older," she said. "So unless I've aged incredibly well, I think it's safe to say that we're still us. So our future selves are around here somewhere."

"I wish we knew how far into the future we went," Samantha murmured as her eyes roamed over the house. "What year is it? That would help us figure out where our future selves might—"

"Who are you?"

Both sisters turned to see a woman in the dining room. She

was young, looked to be about their age, with long black hair that was pulled back away from her face. She wore cutoff jeans and a yellow shirt.

Kathy looked to Samantha, then back at the woman. "Uh…who are you?"

The woman's face furrowed. "Kathy?"

Do you know her? Samantha pinged in Kathy's mind.

Not that I can remember, Kathy thought back. Try searching her mind for any memories that would help us figure out who she is.

Kathy could tell Samantha was quietly focusing her power in the woman's direction. And then the woman seemed to recognize Samantha's probe.

She charged at the sisters and knocked Samantha to the ground. Kathy stepped out of the way and raised her hands to freeze the woman, but she wouldn't freeze.

As if recognizing the attempt at magic, the woman turned to the door, raised her own hands, and the two front doors swung open on their own. Then, with another flick of her hands, Samantha and Kathy both scooted across the hardwood floor toward the threshold.

"Get out of here," the woman said. "And don't come back."

Samantha and Kathy wasted no time getting to their feet and running out into the hot summer sun. Behind them, the doors to their own house slammed shut.

CHAPTER 4

The sisters made it out onto the sidewalk and started walking down the blocks that they knew so well. But just as inside their house, there were subtle differences in this neighborhood from the neighborhood in their own time. Many trees had been cut down, others had grown up considerably, casting new shadows on the street. House colors had changed. Porches added. The cars parked in the driveways all looked sleek and futuristic compared to the boxy ones they were used to in the nineties. As one passed on the street, it cruised along almost silently and Kathy stared with admonishment.

"Hello!" Samantha called up into the sky. "Fates ladies! Come out and tell us what we're supposed to be seeing!"

"What are you doing?" Kathy asked in a hushed tone. It was

her way of trying to get Samantha to stop shouting—and drawing attention to them—on the street. Kathy looked around, worried at who might be listening.

"I'm trying to get the Fates to show themselves so they can explain to us why we're here. What we're supposed to be seeing. They just sent us forward in time without any explanation. Without any guidance. It's *rude.*"

Kathy rolled her eyes. "I don't think they care very much about being rude, Sam. Besides, they told us why we're here. We're supposed to witness the horrific future that we caused by failing to stop a vampire bite."

Samantha gestured around the neighborhood. "Look around, Kathy. Does this look horrific to you? It looks basically the same as it did in our time."

"Maybe on the surface, it does. But there has to be something here that is so bad that the Fates decided to intervene."

"I know, it's just…I never got to say goodbye to Steven and Josh."

"Like the Fates said, they won't know that you disappeared at all."

"Yeah, but *I'll* know. And what if we don't come back?"

Kathy was quiet as she watched her sister study the sidewalk. It was wider than the ones they were used to in their time. Another subtle change.

"You're afraid that there really is something horrific here

and that it'll kill us," Kathy said softly.

Samantha shrugged an admission.

"But the Fates wouldn't let that happen," Kathy said. "They *want* us to stop this. They won't let us die."

"What if our free will puts us in a position where they have no choice but to let it happen?"

"Well." Kathy put her arm around her sister and pulled her close. "We'll just have to make sure that our free will puts us in a position where we're *guaranteed* to go home."

Samantha grabbed her sister's hand that hung on her shoulder and pulled it a little tighter around her own neck. "Thanks. I know I'm being paranoid. It's just that, ever since we went away in October and almost got killed by people who weren't magical at all, I've been very aware of my own mortality and what kind of damage would be done if I wasn't here. I don't want to leave my family too soon."

"And you won't," Kathy said. "Think of this trip to the future as a way to make sure that we go back in time and take the proper steps to create a good future for Josh, and the new baby."

Samantha absently reached for her belly. "Do you think it'd be worthwhile to come up with a ritual to try to summon the Fates? That woman in the house seemed to recognize you. Maybe she's your daughter or something. The magic book could still be in there."

Kathy shook her head. "No. If she was my daughter, I hope that she wouldn't call me by my first name."

"True, but then, it's the future. Anything is possible. Especially if this future is so terrible that we need to change it. If we call on the Fates, maybe they can give us some direction so that we can see what we need to see, go back and stop the bite, and then go home."

"But I don't think that we have the authority—or the power—to summon the Fates. They exist beyond us. Beyond the rules. They're the ones who *make* the rules, right? They can do whatever they want. I think we'd just be wasting our time, even if we *were* successful in summoning them."

"How so?"

"Well, have they given us a straight answer yet?" Kathy asked. "Say we get them here, they'd probably give us some vague, long-winded answer that didn't tell us anything useful."

"So then what do you suggest we do?"

"We were sent forward in time to witness the effects of our misstep, as they put it, right?"

"Yeah, but we haven't seen that yet," Samantha said.

"So let's go find it."

"Where?"

"I have a hunch." Kathy grabbed her sister's hand and pulled her down the sidewalk. "Follow me."

CHAPTER 5

It took nearly an hour, but the sisters finally made it to W 21st Street, where they had witnessed the vampire bite the night before. Or rather, the night before in *their* time. With the summer heat, the girls were sweaty and tired, having been in the sun for so long. Many of the street trees had been cut down. The sidewalks, while mostly wider, were all in terrible, crumbling condition. Still, there seemed to be just as much traffic on the street as there'd always been.

"Okay, we're here." Samantha put her hands on her hips and looked around the neighborhood. "Now what?"

"Now we look for clues that might help us."

"What kind of clues?"

"Well, this is where it happened." Kathy pointed to the

driveway of the house they had visited the night before, an indeterminable number of years ago. The house sat vacant, with spray paint along the siding. The porch roof had collapsed and two of the windows upstairs had been boarded up. The rest had been shattered. Whether it was from vandals or decay, it was hard to tell.

"But why would that matter to vampires?" Samantha asked. "You're assuming they hold sentimental value to this moment."

"I'm *not* saying that," Kathy snapped. The heat and the burning sun was making her agitated faster than she would normally feel. "I'm just trying to look for answers. Maybe I can get a vision from this place or something."

Samantha gestured toward the driveway. "By all means, be my guest. It's probably better if we get out of view of the street anyway." She looked up and down the row of houses. It was quiet. And for the middle of the day in the summer time, that seemed very suspicious. The hair on the back of her neck stood on end.

The sisters moved down the driveway toward the garage. Samantha was getting serious déjà vu coming back to the place they had been not long ago.

Kathy, meanwhile, crouched down and held her hands out to the driveway. The night before it had been covered in snow, now it was bone dry and cracked with age.

"Anything?" Samantha asked.

"No. Maybe we don't have our powers here."

I think we do, Samantha probed into her sister's mind. *I've already used mine before.*

Kathy shot her a look. "Okay. So we do."

"And if we can't get anything from coming here, then we've wasted our time."

Undeterred, Kathy turned her attention to the house. The back door had been boarded up, but it had since been kicked in. Leaves and garbage covered the threshold and carried all the way inside.

"Don't go in there!" Samantha scolded. "You have no idea what's in there and I'm getting a terrible feeling about this neighborhood."

"We came here for answers, so what better place to look than the house where the vampire lived?" Kathy nodded inside and then disappeared inside the house before her sister could protest anymore.

With no other options, Samantha followed Kathy inside.

Immediately, she was hit with the smell of urine and feces. Clearly, squatters and animals alike had been using this house for shelter. And the heat was doing the smell no favors.

They stood in the kitchen, at the back of the house. It had been gutted. Apparently an attempt at a renovation that had been abandoned.

Through a tight doorway, they entered a small room with a beautiful built-in china cabinet. Clearly, this had once been a dining room. And the remnants of the built-in furniture that spoke of prideful homeowners of years gone, now sadly neglected, made Samantha sad. It reminded her of the house she and Steven had visited when she was pregnant with Josh. Back when they considered buying their own fixer-upper.

A cased opening carried them from the dining room to the room at the front of the house. It was dark. The large picture window at the front had been boarded up with plywood carelessly screwed into intricate oak moulding. Still, some sunlight shone through the small windows that framed the fireplace.

"This must've been where the squatters stayed," Kathy whispered. She gestured to the deflated air mattress on the floor, covered with a dirty throw blanket.

"Just be on high alert in case you need to freeze anything," Samantha said.

Kathy nodded then led them to the stairs.

"Are we sure it's safe up there?"

"Only one way to find out."

As they climbed the stairs, the stench of feces grew worse, but Kathy acted as though she didn't smell anything.

Samantha murmured, "Remember when you said we should do things to put us in a position where it's guaranteed that we'll get home?"

Kathy shushed her and stepped across the creaky floorboards. The landing was tight and dark, existing only to serve as an entry point for the upstairs bedrooms and bathroom.

"Are we going to check every bedroom?" Samantha asked. "Because if we find anyone—"

"Would you stop? I'm hoping to get a vision from being in the same house as the man who was bitten, and I'm not going to get one with you complaining the whole time."

Samantha bit back her lip and they continued on.

There were three bedrooms. Each one in various states of decay. Broken glass littered the floor of one, mixed with leaves that had blown in from outside. The next had a mattress in the corner, where another squatter had been sleeping. They bypassed the bathroom, both sisters intentionally looking anywhere but the mess that had collected in the toilet and the bathtub.

The third bedroom had broken glass on the floor as well. In fact, all of the glass from the window had been carefully knocked out. The sisters walked up toward the broken window and saw that it led out onto the roof of the kitchen, which extended out the back of the house.

"Looks like the squatters used this as an entry point for getting into the house," Kathy said. "Before they kicked in the back door, that is."

"Are you sure it was the squatters who did that?"

That statement made the sisters even more terrified of the undefined threat in the future. Until Samantha noticed something through the window.

"Wait, look at that." Samantha pointed out over the tops of the other houses in the neighborhood. With most of the trees having been cut down, their view from the second story was better than it would've been otherwise.

"What is that?"

"It looks like some kind of prison or something." Samantha gaped at the large concrete structure that rose up in the center of the city. She knew for sure that it hadn't been there before. Even the few tall buildings downtown were difficult to see this far away from the city's core.

"Maybe that's the bad thing we were meant to see."

"It looks like it was built by the railroad tracks," Samantha said. "Do you think it could be a train station?"

Kathy shook her head. "I don't think it's as innocent as that."

Samantha was quiet, agreeing wholeheartedly with her sister, but wanting to find some glimmer of hope regardless. "Do you think we should check it out?"

"And do what? Just walk right in and ask to poke around? Sam, you were nervous about walking into this abandoned house, now you want to go into some strange new prison?"

Samantha rolled her eyes. "Okay. So then what do you suggest we do?"

"I say we find our future selves and talk to them. They'll remember coming to the future. Maybe they can point us in the right direction of what we're supposed to see."

"And how do you suggest we find them?"

"We go back to our family home. No matter how bad the future gets, we wouldn't let that house go easily."

"We've already been kicked out of it once," Samantha said. "What happens if that woman sees us lurking outside her house? I'm not really in the mood to be cursed by another witch today."

"Well, then we're going to have to hide, aren't we?"

"You're not doing too good of a job at it."

The voice was deep and harsh, coming from the doorway of the bedroom.

Both sisters spun around and faced the intruder—then were shocked when another man walked in behind him. They had a hungry look in their eyes that made the sisters' stomachs turn.

"Who are you?" Samantha demanded.

"We're the neighborhood watch," the second man said with a sneer.

"Sam…" Kathy pointed to what the men held in their hands. Metal pipes.

Samantha looked both men in the eyes. "We were just looking. Let us go and nobody has to get hurt."

"Ah, but you're already here." The first one slapped the pipe against his palm. He turned to his friend, "What do you say, Graham? You think we should hit them or have fun with them?"

Graham licked his lips. "Been a while since we've had some fun."

The sisters took a step back, their feet sliding on broken glass, and their backs hitting the wall.

They were trapped.

CHAPTER 6

The first man reached for Kathy's hand, but she pulled away before he could get a good grasp. Meanwhile, Graham did the same for Samantha and noticed the glimmer of her wedding ring.

"Oh, this one is taken!" He tried to reach for Samantha again, but she delivered a quick punch in his face that caused his nose to start bleeding. He backed away and held his nose. "You bitch!"

"Kathy, a little help?" Samantha called to her sister.

The first man raised his pipe and started to swing it, just as Kathy put up her hands and froze both men.

Samantha let out a heavy breath of air that she'd been holding. "It's about friggin' time!"

Kathy rolled her eyes. "I needed them to get out of the doorway so we can leave." She eyed up the men, the look of anger still frozen on their faces, and considered taking the pipes from them and hitting them with it. But that wouldn't make her any better than them.

"Whatever," Samantha said. "Let's just get out of here."

Both sisters hurried out of the room, down the stairs, and out of the house. Neither one of them felt any relief until they were safely away from the street. Even then, the prospect of how dangerous the city had become still weighed heavy in their minds.

The sisters were exhausted by the time they made it back to Arlington Road. The sun had drained their energy. Although they had stopped to grab something to eat on the walk back, the single bottle of water that each of them had was barely enough to fully hydrate them in the summer sun.

What was worse, that meal had used up the last of the money that Samantha had had in her pocket. It had been a shock to hear the price of their modest meal. Inflation had wreaked havoc on the economy in this new time. If they didn't get home soon, they would need to find someone to take them in to provide them a place to sleep and something to eat now that they were out of money.

THE FATES

Samantha hoped they would be home much sooner than that.

"Where do you think we should hide out and wait for ourselves to come back home?" Kathy asked.

"Somewhere where we can see the house," Samantha suggested. "Do you think the Kors still live across the street?" She pointed to the large house that sat across from theirs. Much of the landscaping had overgrown, providing many hiding places.

"I don't know. They're pretty old in our time," Kathy said. "It's probably someone new."

"Well, even if it is, do you think they'd care? Look at the house."

Kathy shrugged and they pressed on.

As they settled behind an overgrown bush, Samantha kept her eyes on the house. It was large and weathered. Much different than what they were used to in their time. The Kors took much care in their home, but the one in front of Samantha now was tired. Chipped paint, sagging porch, leaves collecting by the garage doors.

What was it with the future that made everyone neglect their houses?

As she scrutinized the large window in the front of the house, though, she saw no sign of life. Sure, the curtains still hung by the window, but they were sun-faded and worn. Upon closer inspection, she saw a collection of newspapers by the front door.

Abandoned.

Just like the one on W 21st Street.

"Sam, look," Kathy hissed from behind her.

She spun around and peered through the bushes. The chatter of children walking home from school filled the street. Samantha smiled. At least that was the same in the future. She was beginning to feel overwhelmed with all the changes she was encountering.

Two of the kids in particular were walking toward the front door of their house. A girl and her younger brother. The boy looked quite young, as if he was in his first year of school. The girl, meanwhile, was quite a few years older.

"Any guess who they are?" Kathy asked.

Samantha shrugged as she watched the kids disappear into the house. "No idea."

"Do you think another family moved in? Maybe that's how the woman recognized me. Maybe it was from the house closing or something."

"No, we wouldn't sell the family home. No matter how bad things get. Not after we worked so hard to keep it." She thought back to the countless hours she and Kathy had spent working to scrape by enough cash to pay the bills.

"Then who are those people?" Kathy asked.

"I don't know," Samantha admitted. "But there's only one way to find out, and that's to watch the house. Maybe we'll start to piece it together when we see ourselves come home."

"But what if we don't?" Kathy suggested. "What if, in this

version of the future, we're both dead? Maybe that woman inside recognized me because of an old photo album or something that was left in the house when they bought it."

"Yeah, but she threw us out of the house using *magic*. We've run into other witches in Erie, sure, but what are the odds one of them buys the house after we've died? If you ask me, we're still alive in this time. And I'm willing to bet that we still live in that house."

"With those strangers?"

"Maybe they're not strangers to our future selves."

"So what do you suggest we do?"

"We still need allies who will help us get answers," Samantha said. "And I think the best allies we'll be able to find is ourselves. So we just need to wait for us to come home."

"And what happens if we don't?"

"If we don't show up by nightfall, then we come up with a Plan B."

Kathy raised her eyebrows, then relented. She sank down onto the grass and peered through the bushes.

They could be in for a long wait.

CHAPTER 7

Dusk filled the sky, and yet the air was still warm. The sisters remained perched behind the bush. Kathy had begun to doze off, while Samantha watched, hoping that the lights inside the house would come on and better reveal the actions of those inside.

They still hadn't seen their future selves come back, and Samantha was growing nervous that they wouldn't be able to find an ally in this time, and they wouldn't be able to see what the Fates had sent them forward in time to see. And if they didn't see it, would they be stuck in the future forever? Would the Fates just leave them there and forget about them?

Kathy jerked as she tried to prevent herself from falling asleep. She sat up straight and looked around. "Have you seen anything?"

"Nothing since we saw that man come home a little while ago," Samantha said. The young man had long hair, that was pulled back in a bun. He pulled up in a pickup truck loaded with tools.

"Any idea who he is?"

Samantha shrugged. "Maybe Josh. Hopefully Josh. Should we go in and try to introduce ourselves to him?" She had been debating that idea with herself for the last hour, since he came home. But she held firm that they were going to stay put until theirselves came home. Approaching the man she hoped to be her son would have to be the Plan B she had mentioned earlier, because, of course, she didn't actually *have* a Plan B in place.

"Maybe. Has anyone left?"

Samantha shook her head. "No. And what's weirder is that I haven't seen *anyone* leave any of the houses, all down the street. People are coming home, sure, but nobody else is going anywhere. They're just locking themselves in their houses."

Kathy scrunched her face. "Are you sure? Maybe you missed something." She peered over the bush and looked down the block, then in the other direction. "Every house has a car in the driveway."

"Except the ones that are empty."

"And I don't smell any grills or barbecues."

"And I don't hear any kids playing outside," Samantha added. "Kathy, this is weird. It's a perfectly gorgeous summer night and not a single person is enjoying it? I mean, is one of the changes of that vampire bite endless summer all the time? Maybe everyone's used to this weather. Maybe it's *actually* January and there's been some cosmic shift that creates summer-like temperatures all year round?"

Kathy shook her head. "You know that's not the case. That doesn't even make sense!"

"None of this makes sense!" Then Samantha noticed two men coming down the middle of the street. She ducked down lower and peered through the bush. "There. There's two people right now."

"See?" Kathy said. "Nothing to worry about."

"Shh! Let's just watch them. See how they act."

The two men continued on in the middle of the street. That alone was odd, but then, as Samantha watched them closer, she saw that they weren't walking at all. They were *floating*. Inches above the ground.

"Vampires," Samantha whispered to her sister. They were huddled close, so she didn't have to raise her voice very loud.

Yet the two men had heard her. At the sound of her voice, they stopped in their tracks. In a quick ninety-degree turn, the men faced the bush and began floating toward them, moving only enough the get over the curb and onto the sidewalk.

Samantha rose, pulling Kathy to her feet beside her.

"Freeze them!" Samantha called to her sister as they took a step back.

Kathy put up her hands, but one of the vampires waved his

hand out, smacking the younger sister in the face and knocking her to the ground.

Samantha wanted to rush to her sister's aid, but she didn't want to turn her back to the vampires, who now outnumbered her. "Kathy, are you okay?"

Her sister groaned. "Yeah. Just peachy."

"Stand down, witch," one of the vampires said.

Samantha curled her lip. "You really know nothing about witches, do you?" Focusing on his mind, she tried to find his deepest fear and bring it to the surface. But the only thing that seemed to be on his mind was to follow through with his orders to patrol the streets.

What world were they in?

The pause gave the vampire enough time to knock her to the ground with a hard slap as well.

Soon, both sisters lay on the ground beside each other as the two vampires towered over them.

The vampires' skin was so pale. In the growing darkness, it seemed to almost glow, like a full moon. They carried no weapons, although one of them held some sort of small technological device.

"What are your names?" the one without the device asked.

The sisters rose to the feet, but he seized their arms with his hands. His skin was icy cold, and his hold was strong, almost painful.

"Uh…"

"What is your reasoning for violating curfew?" the other vampire asked.

"Curfew?" Kathy looked to her sister, then back at the vampires. "We're adults. We don't have a curfew."

There was no hint of humor in the vampires' faces. No sign of any emotion at all.

"Everyone has a curfew," the one with the device said. He slipped it in his pocket, then took hold of Kathy's arm so that the other one could hold both of Samantha's arms behind her back.

"Since you refuse to identify yourself, you will be taken into custody, where you will be assigned a hearing to plead your case."

"Custody?" Samantha blurted. "*Jail*? You're taking us to jail for staying out late?" She dug her heels in the ground to try to stop him from taking her, but the vampire was too strong and he simply pulled her along.

"You can't do this!" Kathy pleaded as she tried to fight off her restrainer. "Don't you have to read us our rights? Don't you have to provide us a lawyer?"

Neither vampire answered their questions. Like machines, they carried the witches away, down the street, where they saw faces in several windows, peering out as they were carted away.

CHAPTER 8

"We're sorry. The number you have dialed is not in service." The robotic voice rang out on the other end of the phone.

Samantha pulled the phone from her ear and stared at it. The number she had dialed was displayed on the screen in front of her. She had dialed the house number correctly. How was it not in service?

The vampires had given her one phone call. A courtesy, although Samantha was willing to bet that they'd do everything in their power to stall any attorneys or other representation if Samantha *had* called for them.

She had decided to try her chances with the house, hoping that whomever picked up would offer her mercy. But if she couldn't even reach them…

"All done?" The vampire guard who was in the room took the phone from Samantha's hand and placed it back in the cradle. Then, with a firm hand, he guided her back to the interrogation room.

In typical cop-show style, there was a lone table with a single chair on one side and two chairs on the other. On the side with the double chairs was a large mirror, that Samantha knew had people watching on the other side.

"But I didn't even get through to anyone," she said.

The vampire closed the door and took a seat at the table, then motioned for Samantha to take hers across from him. "We can try again later. My name is Detective Dante Wilhelm. And your name is…?"

"*Detective*?" she blurted. "But there's been no crime!"

He scribbled on his notepad, seemingly disinterested in the conversation. His skin was just as white as the men who had pulled her and Kathy off the street. Apparently even the police force was full of vampires in this world. "Violating curfew."

"So a detective's getting involved because we stayed out a little late?" Her mind was spinning. What was going on? How did the vampires get this much control?

Detective Wilhelm glared at her through his eyebrows, then softened his stance as he sat back in his chair. Tossing his pen on the table, he crossed his arms. "The curfew law is in place to protect residents. You never know what kind…*dangers* are lurking at night."

Samantha suspected the only danger out at night were other vampires like him. She wondered how often people—or whole families, even—disappeared without a trace in the middle of the night. By instituting a curfew, it allowed the vampires to move freely during a period where they knew they wouldn't be spotted committing horrifying crimes.

But she was jumping to conclusions.

"What about if I made a…*magical* call?" That was a risk, revealing that she was a witch. But then, since Detective Wilhelm was a vampire, she knew that he knew a thing or two about magic himself.

"So you're a witch?"

Samantha narrowed her eyes. She *was* a witch. A witch with the power of telepathy. She focused that power and probed into Detective Wilhelm's mind. The first thing that jumped out to her on the surface was the date: 2022. That meant that she and Kathy were thirty-one years into the future. The next thing that jumped out to her—

Her head jerked back as a splitting headache hit her hard. She pinched the bridge of her nose and squeezed her eyes shut.

"*Don't* do that again," Wilhelm warned.

When she opened her eyes, she saw that he was leaning over the table now, his finger pointing in her face. He settled back into his seat, then returned to his notepad. He tried to play off her attempt at probing his mind, but she could tell that it bothered him. Angered him.

"Now," he moved on, "why were you violating curfew?"

Samantha decided silence was her best path forward. No matter what she said, her words would crucify her somehow in this unjust reality she found herself in. Better if she didn't give any fuel to the fire. She suspected they would eventually give up and either leave her alone or put her in a jail cell. There, she could use her telepathy to try to find Kathy and figure out a way out of the prison.

"Can you at least tell me your name?" he asked.

Samantha crossed her arms. She ignored her throbbing head.

After another moment of silence, Wilhelm slammed the pad of paper on the table, then stood and came around to Samantha's side. He grabbed her by the arm hard and dragged her out of the room.

She resisted the urge to ask where he was taking her, although her mind swam with panic. He led her through a crowded room, then down a long corridor lined with cinder blocks. Eventually, they made it through a door with a guard outside. He waved a badge, the door clicked, then the guard opened it for Wilhelm and Samantha to pass.

They stepped into a prison block, where people lay quietly on their cots behind steel bars. When they got to an empty one, another guard was there to unlock it for Wilhelm and he shoved

Samantha inside, slamming the bars closed behind her.

"Maybe some time in here will help you think of something to say." After another murderous glare in her direction, he disappeared back toward the central office of the prison.

CHAPTER 9

Kathy was starting to drift off in her cot in her prison cell. She was freezing. The whole prison had no heat and the cinder blocks seemed to suck away any warmth at all. Even though outside was balmy and warm, Kathy had goosebumps up and down her arms and she shivered under the thin sheet on the cot.

She had had her time in the interrogation room, where she had offered nothing of substance to the interrogator. Detective Wilhelm. He seemed particularly agitated when he came in to talk to her, and that gave her a sign that she shouldn't offer him any piece of useful information. In fact, all she did was return his questions with more questions.

"What is your name?"

"Why am I here?"

THE FATES

"What were you doing out so late?"

"What charges are you holding me on?"

"Where do you live?"

"Where do *you* live?"

After throwing some of his questions back at him and refusing to answer any of them, he had thrown her in the prison cell and told her he'd be back later to talk to her, or to convince her to talk to him.

The *convincing* part was what scared her about what was to come. It had taken her a while to calm down, especially as more and more people were brought into the prison for violating curfew.

Kathy. Samantha's voice pinged in her head.

Sam? Kathy thought back.

Finally! I've been head-hopping for the last hour trying to find you! Are you okay?

Sometimes, having a telepathic sister came in handy for situations like these. And, unfortunately, they often found themselves in situations like these.

I'm fine. Just cold. And tired. They haven't given me anything to eat, either.

Probably not until we talk, Samantha pinged in her mind. *Did you tell them anything?*

No. Did you?

Nope.

Good. We're not going to stick around long enough to give

them another chance to get us to talk, are we?

Hell no! We're getting out of here!

Any ideas how? Kathy had been trying to piece that together for a while. Even if they managed to get out of the prison cell, they had no idea where to go once they got out of the prison block, and no way to get out onto the street safely without being caught. Sure, they could try a spell, but then what?

We're going to have to use magic, Samantha thought back. *Your power in particular. I tried mine on the detective who interviewed me and he caught on and fought back.*

Are you okay?

I'm fine, but I'm not interested in trying that again. Kathy, we need to find our future selves. They'll definitely remember coming to this time and maybe they can tell us when the Fates pull us back to our own time and what they want us to see.

I'm surprised they haven't pulled us back to our time already, Kathy thought. *This is clearly a future that we don't want.*

Yeah, but I'm still having a hard time believing that one vampire bite led to all of this.

Well, believe it, because right now we're trapped.

I know. That's why if we get out of here and find our future selves, they can help convince those people in our house that we're the good guys too, Samantha pinged. *Maybe those people are our children.*

Except that girl called me Kathy *and not Aunt* Kathy *or Mom.*

Maybe the whole "aunt" and "uncle" thing just doesn't suit her? Anyway, your freezing power is going to need to get us out of here.

Kathy had been afraid of that. She knew that it would be the most useful, but she had no idea where she was running to once she got out and she only hoped that she'd be able to freeze any other danger that she encountered long enough so that she didn't get trapped again. The only thing worse than being held prisoner was being caught for trying to *escape* imprisonment.

And how will I find you? Kathy asked in her thoughts.

I'll be in your head the whole time, guiding you.

Kathy admitted to herself that she liked that. And, now that she thought it, she knew her sister knew it too.

Sometimes, having a sister who was telepathic was a pain in the ass.

Hey! Samantha said in Kathy's head. *I may be a pain in the ass sometimes, but you need me if we're going to break out of this place.*

Okay, but they're vampires, Sam. They know a thing or two about magic themselves. They've probably put some precautions in place to prevent witches from escaping.

Well, until we're up against them, we have no way of knowing. Clearly, our powers still work in this time. So we'll need to use that to our advantage. Are you ready?

Not really.

Good! Let's go!

CHAPTER 10

After devising a plan with Samantha telepathically, Kathy hung out by the steel bars at the front of her cell and waited for the perfect opportunity. She watched as the guards made their patrols up and down the corridor, which was wide enough so that they couldn't be grabbed by prisoners.

The guards didn't carry any weapons. The fact that they floated a few inches from the floor and their pasty-white skin told her that they were vampires too. Must be the only way that the regime could recruit people to fight for their cause.

Down the corridor, Kathy spotted a guard coming her way. She tucked behind the wall so that he didn't see her. Then she closed her eyes and tried to sense his presence coming up behind her.

THE FATES

When she did, she put her hand out and froze him when he was right in front of her.

The keys hung from a rung on his belt loop. She had to press herself against the bars of her cell in order to reach the keys, and even then she had to finagle them until they were free of him.

It took longer than she expected and her arms strained against the confines of the steel bars. She was afraid that he would unfreeze at any moment and snatch her arm. Against the steel bars, her bones would snap easily.

Finally, she freed the keys, just as the guard unfroze. He didn't seem to notice at first until the keys jangled in Kathy's hands. He stopped, looked at her, then looked down at the keys. What had happened didn't quite seem to register with him at first and Kathy used that to her advantage to find the right key, which wasn't hard to do. It was a simple skeleton key, and matched the keyhole in her cell perfectly.

By the time she swung the door open, the guard had barked for backup down the corridor, then took a step toward Kathy.

She hopped back, then spun around and drove her foot up into the guard's face. He toppled back to the floor and she sprinted out of her cell and down the corridor.

At the end, coming from the door, several other vampires emerged.

"Help me!" one of the other prisoners called to her.

"Just toss me the keys!" another suggested.

"Hey, you can't just leave us all in here!"

"Run! Save yourself!"

"Watch out for the guards! They'll turn you into one of them!"

The cries from the other prisoners were defeating, only making it more stressful as Kathy ran for her life and judged all of the potential dangers she was about to encounter.

She waited until the last guard had come through the door to freeze them, stopping all of the guards in their tracks and propping the door open as well.

She came up on the men and started to maneuver around their frozen forms, but jumped when the prison alarm went off. Quickly regaining her composure, she picked her way around the guards and made it through the door, which led to a concrete stairwell.

More guards rushed up the stairs from the floor below and she froze them too, working her way around them and down onto the cell block below her.

I'm about five cells in front of the door by the staircase, Samantha pinged in Kathy's head.

Got it, Kathy thought back.

She burst through the door into the lower cell block and raced along the deserted corridor. Most of the guards had cleared out to run to the alarm blaring on the second story, which gave Kathy some time to find Samantha's cell.

But not much.

"Kathy!" Samantha called from a few cells down.

THE FATES

Kathy rushed to her sister and pulled the keys out. The lock on Samantha's door looked different, and it took several precious seconds to find the right key. When she did, though, they two of them swung open the door and quickly embraced.

"Thanks," Samantha said.

They joined hands and raced down the corridor in the opposite direction of the stairs, toward the central offices of the prison.

The door at the end opened and two more vampires emerged. Samantha stopped in her tracks, bringing Kathy to a halt with her. The younger witch put up her free hand and froze the two guards, then tugged on her sister's arm with her other hand and carefully led her out into the center of the building.

The alarms on the wall were flashing red and blaring loudly, creating chaos and panic. The witches used that to their advantage to sneak into a room just off of the door leading to the prison cells.

The room they stepped into was dark, and Kathy kept the door opened only a crack to allow light in, and to watch to see if anyone would discover them. She had to be ready in case she needed to freeze.

Outside the room, more guards rushed in to assist with the prison break.

This looks like a utility room, Samantha said in Kathy's head. It was better to communicate wordlessly.

Any exits?

Not that I can see—wait a minute! This looks like a trash chute. It has to lead outside.

Or straight into an incinerator, Kathy fired back. She heard voices outside, but she couldn't place who they were or what exactly they were saying over the deafening alarm and commotion out in the hall.

I don't think they would use an incinerator, Samantha pinged. *Even in this part of the prison it's freezing. Vampires don't need heat to stay warm. They're dead—or* un*dead, rather.*

Your point?

I think we'll be safe if we jump.

Kathy still wasn't sure. They had no way of knowing what lay on the other side of that trash chute. They might end up in a worse situation than they were currently. Although, judging by what she saw outside, she wasn't sure they could be in a *worse* situation.

"Make sure all the gates are locked down!" she heard a male voice shout outside their hiding place. "We want to keep them inside the prison walls!"

Then, just outside the door, another voice said, "We'll have to check every room. They must be hiding someplace around here."

Kathy turned to her sister in the darkness. All other fears she had moments ago were gone, exchanged for the fear that they would be caught. "Through the chute. Go!"

"You hear that?" the voice on the other side of the door said.

THE FATES

Seconds later, the door burst open, just as the sisters were climbing into the trash chute. Samantha jumped first, followed by Kathy, who slipped down into the cramped darkness as the vampire reached for her.

CHAPTER 11

The trip down the trash chute was like a terrifying, smelly, dirty water slide without the water. It was a tight space and the sisters slammed against the sides of the metal walls the whole way down. Dust kicked up in their faces as their bodies were slammed against mysterious sticky and wet substances lining the chute.

Finally, they were deposited onto a pile of garbage bags. Something within the bags crunched when they landed, but mostly the bags were soft cushions that broke their fall.

Neither of the girls moved at first after being deposited at the bottom of the chute. Both lay back as they recuperated from the torment they just subjected their bodies to.

"Who's idea was it to go down the trash chute?" Samantha groaned.

"Yours."

"Oh yeah." She looked around at the trash pile they lay in. Piles of black garbage bags, like any other dump they'd seen before. The only oddity was that this was in the middle of the city. "Any ideas what we do now?"

"Get as far away from this prison as we can." Kathy started to climb down the pile of trash bags, but stopped when she felt Samantha's hand on her shoulder.

"Look over there."

The trash dump was just outside the walls of the prison. If they moved quickly, they could escape before the guards were on them.

But then Kathy noticed what else Samantha had been pointing at. The area surrounding the prison was almost unrecognizable. It was Erie, that was for sure, but everything looked more tired. Houses were run down, other blocks of neighborhoods had been ripped out, trees cut down, sidewalks cracked, the street completely empty of any signs of life.

Looming up along the waterfront in the distance was a large Romanesque building, closer to downtown, that very much hadn't been there in their time.

"The vampires have taken over," Kathy murmured. "Is this the result of that vampire bite we were supposed to prevent?"

"Apparently." Samantha still had a hard time believing it.

"Well, I don't like it."

"Neither do I. And neither do the Fates. Otherwise they

wouldn't have sent us here."

"But why haven't they pulled us back yet? Haven't we seen enough? What more is there to see? This is definitely not a future I want to have."

"I think they want us to see—and feel—the gravity of the situation to make sure that we stop all of this from happening."

Kathy rolled her eyes. As far as she was concerned, the lesson had been learned. Apparently, the Fates thought different. "So what do we do in the meantime? We can't just let the vampires take us prisoner."

"We need to do what we've always done. Find a way to stop them."

"How? I think that's a losing battle." "Sure it is, but unless we want to end up in there—" Samantha pointed to a building beside them with a large smokestack that was billowing out into the air. Judging from the revolting scent filling the air, it was no doubt that they were burning bodies. "—we have to try."

"I just don't understand how it could've gotten so bad."

"I don't know, either. But we need to find out. This is not the Erie that I want for my children."

CHAPTER 12

The girls ran down the deserted streets as fast as they could. The nighttime darkness enveloped them since a lot of the street lights had been blown out. The sirens from the prison behind them were growing fainter, but it was still loud, ringing out throughout the eerily quiet neighborhoods. If there had been anyone living in the vicinity surrounding the prison, it would surely wake them up.

In the deeper recesses of the shadows, they began to see vampires appearing. None of them began chasing them, or making an effort to. Yet. Instead, they just watched them go. Keeping tabs on them. It was almost creepier that they were just letting the girls pass. As if they were running into a trap.

"Should we change directions?" Kathy murmured in a

ragged breath as they ran.

Samantha, who had a splitting cramp in her side, was too breathless to respond with words. *Blue house up ahead on the left. Run through the yard, hop the fence, and high-tail it over to the next street.*

Do you think you have it in you to do all that?

Do we have a choice?

There was no time for a response. They made the sudden change in course, darted down a cracked driveway with two forgotten cars parked on it. Samantha whipped open the gate in the chain-link fence and ran through, then dove through the few missing slats from the wooden fence in the back of the yard. They burst through the yard of the house on the other side, hopped on the hood of another abandoned car, and came out onto the next street.

Once back on the street, they saw more vampires lurking. This time, up ahead, they began to close in on the sisters. Both girls slowed, then retreated backwards, looking for another place to escape to.

Kathy began to pull her sister down the driveway of another house, but stopped when she came face-to-face with a glowing-white vampire.

They sprinted in another direction and nearly collided with yet another. When they turned, they saw that the vampires were closing in on them. Surrounding them.

What do we do? Kathy shouted in her head.

Can you freeze them?

And then what? Run? You sound like you're dying, and what if more of them show up? I can't freeze them all.

The vampires formed a tighter ring around the sisters. Several of them hissed at the girls, but none of them moved in to strike. The anticipation was almost worse than the attack.

Almost.

The group suddenly parted and Detective Wilhelm stepped into view.

"I knew from the moment I saw you girls in interrogation that you were trouble," he said.

Don't say anything, Samantha warned her sister. *The worst thing they can do to us is throw us back in prison.*

We escaped their prison, Sam. They're going to do much worse than that!

"Let's see, first you violate curfew, then you escape prison." He tutted three times with his tongue. "We can't let you girls commit anymore crimes, now, can we?"

"Are you a detective, or a judge?" Kathy asked.

Kathy! Samantha scolded with her power. *Don't say anything!*

Wilhelm smirked. "The rules might be firm, but our roles are a little…ambiguous. I can do whatever is necessary in order to maintain the rules."

"So what is the punishment that you're going to dole out?" Samantha asked, realizing immediately she had violated her own vow of silence. As she stared at the authoritative vampire, she forced herself to keep her breathing in check, although she knew that it was impossible. Not only was her heart racing from the sprint, but she was terrified. It was beating so hard that she felt as if it was going to bounce right out of her chest.

"After two serious violations, the violator gets two options: die, or spend the rest of eternity as part of the vampiric army."

Samantha's eyes widened. "That's how you've gained such a following!"

"If you can't beat them, make them join you." He screwed up his face in mock confusion. "Or is that not how that saying goes?" He bared his teeth, with the long incisors showing proudly, and stepped toward them. "Now, who wants the honor of going first?"

"Wait!" Kathy said. "Don't we get to choose whether we want to die or join you?"

Wilhelm stopped and nodded. "You're right. That is customary. But we've never had anyone escape the prison before. So since you're the exception, I'll have to make an exception here regarding your choice. You *will* be joining our army. And you, my dear, will go first. Can't have you freezing anything else."

Kathy felt another vampire grab her arms and hold her back, while a second vampire grabbed her head, holding it back to expose her neck. Two more vampires did the same to Samantha.

THE FATES

"Wait!" Samantha cried. "Take me! I'm the oldest!"

Wilhelm ignored her. He bared his teeth again and leaned in to Kathy's neck. She felt his teeth touch her skin. Then, in a swirl of bright lights, the sisters were gone.

CHAPTER 13

When the sisters reappeared, they were suddenly standing in their house. Only, they knew right away that they weren't back in their time. Instead of Steven and Josh standing before them, it was the woman they had seen in the house before when they had first arrived in the future, and the man they had seen come home from work a couple hours earlier.

"Aunt Kathy!" the man shouted. Then, "Mom?"

The man stepped over the circle of silver candles that surrounded the sisters and wrapped his arms tight around Samantha. She leaned into his strong embrace, feeling the love and warmth radiate off his body, even if he felt like a complete stranger to her. Although, deep inside, she felt a connection to him.

When he pulled away, he was teary-eyed, but he turned and quickly wiped them away, embarrassed by the show of emotion.

"Josh?" Samantha asked hesitantly. She truly had no idea who this man was, but he clearly loved her very much. It had to be her son.

He shook his head and a piece of his long hair fell into his face. He absently tucked it back behind his ear. "No. I'm Chris. Josh's younger brother."

"Chris…" Samantha put her hand to her belly. She couldn't help but smile. "I just found out I was pregnant last month. And now…I'm meeting you as an adult." She stared at him with a newfound perspective, trying to take in the magnitude of meeting her child as a grown adult, but feeling a bit of sensory overload. She felt lightheaded, but her feet were firmly planted on the floor, preventing her from tipping.

"Unless you have a third kid," Kathy offered.

Chris shook his head. "No. Just me and Josh. You're…you're from the past?"

Kathy nodded. "Yeah. It's a long story. Basically, we didn't stop something that should've been stopped, so we were brought to the future to see the disaster we caused so that we can go *back* in time to undo it."

Both Chris and the woman stared at them, trying to decipher if they were being fed the truth.

"Where is Josh?" Samantha asked, trying to get the conversation away from dangerous territory. She and Kathy needed help if they were going to outlive the vampires.

Chris and the woman exchanged looks, then he said, "This is Holly. My wife."

Samantha noted the sudden change in conversation, but stepped over the circle of candles herself and extended her hand toward Holly.

The young witch took a step back and refused to take her hand. "You may have convinced my husband of who you are, but I still have my doubts."

"Understandable," Kathy said. "But if you can't trust us, why did you save us?"

"Because you're family," Chris explained.

"We don't know that," Holly told him. "We've been fooled before."

"But not like this!" he shot back. "Trust me, Holly, I *know* who they are!"

"And what happens if you're wrong?" she asked.

"Okay!" Samantha cut in. "Okay, that's enough. I agree, you guys need to triple-check." She cast a look at Kathy. "Trust us, we've been fooled by family before too."

"So how are we supposed to prove this?" Chris asked. "If you're still pregnant with me, then you don't know anything about me. You haven't even met me!"

Samantha's head was swimming. Her feet suddenly didn't feel so firm anymore and she reached out for something to hold on to. "I think…I think I need to sit down." She used the walls as supports to help her over to the living room. Soon, Kathy was by her side and Chris was on her other side, helping her over to the couch.

"Are you okay?" Chris asked.

She nodded. "I'll be fine." She looked up at Holly. "So how are we going to prove to you that we're trustworthy?"

Holly shrugged, seemingly unconvinced that she could ever trust them.

"Well, since we don't know *you*, maybe you can answer questions about *us*," Kathy suggested. "I mean, you must've heard stories about us for years. And since we've lived those stories, we would know."

Another shrug, this time in acknowledgement.

"Who was your husband?" Chris asked his mother.

Samantha noted the use of past tense. Did that speak to divorce, or death? She swallowed, trying to push down her emotions. "Well, I'm married to your father. Steven Harper."

"And what year did you get married?" he asked.

"That's easy. It's actually our two-year anniversary in our time. We got married in 1989."

"So you're from 1991?" he asked.

Samantha nodded.

"I was born in 1991."

She smiled and put her hand on her belly again. "That would make sense, yeah. When were you—"

"Sam," Kathy warned with a gentle shake of her head.

"Sorry. I don't want to spoil the future."

"This is stupid," Holly declared. "None of this proves anything!"

"We can trust them, Holly!" Chris said. "After all, who would be stupid enough to break out of a vampire prison? We watched them with the location ritual! We watched the whole thing happen!"

"Is that why you saved us?" Kathy asked.

He shrugged. "You were in a bind and we wanted more time to see if you were trustworthy."

"And…?" Samantha asked Holly.

She glared at the sisters, then turned back to her husband.

"Oh, come on!" Chris said, growing agitated. "You can't deny that this Kathy looks like *our* Kathy."

Again, Samantha noted the omission of her own name. Where was she in this future?

Holly studied Kathy, then relented. "Yes, she looks the same. Younger, even. Just like she says. But a shapeshifter—"

"A shapeshifter would take the form of me from *your* time," Kathy said. "Not a version of me from the nineties."

"But how is it possible that you're here?" Holly took a seat on the arm of the chair. A more casual stance. A small victory, but a victory nonetheless. "The Kathy we know is in New York on a business trip."

Kathy smiled and sat up straighter. "I have business in New York?"

The Fates

"We're from the past," Samantha said before they could be given anymore information about their lives in the future. "From 1991, like we said. The Fates sent us forward into the future to see how much evil has spread as a result of us losing one battle with a vampire."

Holly scoffed. "Well, since the city is taken over by a vampiric army, I think it's safe to say that the Fates have a point."

"Yeah, we see that now," Kathy said. "The question is, are you willing to help us?"

"Help you do what?" Holly asked. "If the Fates brought you here, *they* need to send you back."

"Unless we're stuck," Samantha said. "The Fates wouldn't want us to die, and we've almost died several times tonight."

"But you didn't," she said. "And the Fates would know that."

"Look, they need our help, so we need to help," Chris said to his wife. "There's no question. They're family."

"What about *our* family, Christopher?" Holly countered. "We have two kids sleeping upstairs and harboring fugitives is a sure way to get *us* locked up. And *then* what happens to the kids?"

Samantha's eyebrows shot up. "Your...*kids*? I'm a...a *grandmother*?" She felt her head go light again.

Chris crossed his arms and cast a look in his wife's direction. "We're parents, yes. But I don't want to reveal too much. I don't want to alter this world we live in."

"The one with vampires controlling everything?" Kathy

asked. "I'm sorry, but the Fates sent us here to see how terrible this life is for everyone so we can go back and change it. Potentially, all of this will be different by the time we get to this time naturally. What year *is* it anyway?"

"It's 2022," Chris said.

"So what is that…thirty-one years away from our time?" Kathy asked. "A lot can change. For the better, if we're successful. But what we need from you guys is to find a way home. Now I'm paranoid that something's happened to the Fates."

"You think something happened to them?" Samantha asked.

She shrugged. "Well, you never know. Besides, we've seen that this world sucks already. We've already decided it needs to change. Why haven't they pulled us back yet? What are they waiting for?"

"Maybe there's something else we need to see."

Kathy shook her head. "I've seen enough." She turned to Chris and Holly, focusing her attention on the latter. "So, are you willing to help us? This will take a lot of magic. Magic that has to be stronger than ours from thirty years ago. Magic like yours."

Holly nodded. "I think we can try to find a way to get you back home. If you can fix this world we've brought our children into, I'll do anything to make it better for them."

CHAPTER 14

Even though it was thirty years in the future, Samantha felt just at home in the kitchen as she did back in her time. The contents of the black cauldron on the stove bubbled and steamed as she chopped up herbs and other ingredients to add to the potion.

She got the sense that Chris wasn't one for the fine arts of witchcraft. She had no idea what his power was, but judging by the fact that his arms were muscled and toned and his hands were calloused, she guessed that he liked being in the middle of the action as a witch.

And, as a mother, that terrified her. But then, if he was here thirty years later then he had so far succeeded in avoiding destruction. Not that that put her mind at ease at all.

The danger was still there.

"Hand me that mugwort," she asked him.

His eyes surveyed the selection on the table, then he found the bowl she was looking for and handed it to her.

She smirked at him. Even if he didn't seem adept in the kitchen, he at least knew his herbs. "Thanks."

"Any idea what kind of potion you're making?" he asked.

"Something that will thin the lines of space and time," she said. "The potion will, in a sense, prep the universe to accept the spell Kathy and Holly come up with."

"And you think that'll do it? This seems like a big magical task. I know you said that each generation of magic is stronger than the last, but this seems out of reach."

She averted her eyes. "Half of magic is the confidence of believing that something is possible. So I suggest you change your perspective." She passed him back the bowl, then pointed to the bubbling concoction. "Stir that. I want to start on these dishes."

"You can leave them," he said. "If we send you back in time and you make changes that'll alter the future, the dishes in the sink are the least of our concerns."

"I know, but I need to keep my hands busy." She pulled up her sleeves and turned on the faucet. It was the same porcelain sink, but there was a new all-black fixture that made the kitchen look fresh. The little things surprised her each time she stumbled upon another new change.

The Fates

To her back, Chris stood at the pot and stirred. "So you're pregnant with me right now?"

Samantha smiled. "Yeah. Just found out. Actually, I think in this time you're older than I am in my time."

He let out a quiet chuckle. "That's so wild to me. I just turned thirty-one."

"A July baby?"

"Yeah. Did I reveal too much?"

"No. That's my due date anyway. I just hate being *that* pregnant in the summer. When I was pregnant with your brother I was miserable, and he wasn't born until the end of December!"

"I can't even imagine. Holly said she was just uncomfortable during both of her pregnancies. Nothing crazy."

"That's good."

They were quiet. The only sounds were the boiling potion and the running water from the sink.

Samantha's mind was racing with questions. She wanted to know all of the answers of her future, and the fact that those answers were so close—right there, with her adult son—was tempting.

But at the same time, what made life great were the surprises that came up when you were least expecting them. And if those surprises were revealed, then how would she feel going through life knowing what was going to happen? Or worse, would she make different decisions—her *free will*, as the

Fates put it—if she knew what was going to happen, and thus change the future that she thought she knew?

Still, the temptation was too great.

"So, where am I?" she blurted. "In this time?" She chanced a look over her shoulder.

Chris remained facing the boiling pot. "Not here."

"Well, I know that, but am I on a trip with Kathy? Am I staying with Josh somewhere? Are your father and I on a whirlwind vacation?"

He kept quiet, absently stirring the potion with the wooden spoon.

Samantha felt dread come over her, but she forced herself to remain optimistic. He hadn't said anything one way or another. No sense in jumping to conclusions. "What about your father? Where is he?"

"Haven't heard from him in a long while."

Well, there was an answer. Not a particularly good one. If Chris hadn't heard from his father, did that mean that Samantha had had a falling out with her son too? Or did it mean something else entirely?

She swallowed, her mouth suddenly dry. "And Josh? Where's he living nowadays?"

"Mom, you know I can't tell you that," he said. "I can't tell you anything."

She turned and finally met his eyes. "Not even the names of my grandchildren?"

He shook his head. "Not if it's going to change anything, no. This is my life. And you being here could disrupt all of that. For better or worse, this is the world I've always known. You can't just pick and choose which things you can change and which things you keep. As much as I might want to. I have a family. I need to protect them. I know you understand what that feels like."

Samantha nodded, then slowly turned back to the dishes. She hated that Chris had avoided her questions. Worse, she hated upsetting him. But the lack of answers was driving her wild. Especially when faced with evidence that suggested outcomes that she didn't like.

"You've had a lot of loss in your life, haven't you?" she murmured.

Chris was quiet, and when she looked over her shoulder again toward him, she saw the tears in the corners of his eyes. All he could do was nod.

"There's no way to prevent that, is there?"

He swallowed, and then, in a croaky voice, said, "If you *were* able to change the future, there are some things I'd *love* to be able to fix." He shook his head. "But I think even that is out of our hands."

CHAPTER 15

"I think that should do it," Holly said when they had finished writing the spell. "We've conveyed the need and identified the power source, and it all rhymes—you know how magic likes rhymes."

Kathy smirked. "That's true. You're pretty good at this witch stuff, aren't you?"

She nodded. "I've had to be, with the life we lead. And, not to mention, it is a calling for me. I love it. I feel at peace when I'm doing magic. I feel like myself."

"That's good." Kathy felt the same way.

They were sitting on the floor in the living room, their legs stretched out under the coffee table, and their backs against the couch. Two pads of paper and pens lay on the table in front of them. They had taken notes from each of their attempts and combined them to make the final spell.

"So this is your life?" Kathy asked. "Having a demon or someone threaten you, then trying to find a way to kill it, then succeeding in that only to have the next one show up and do it all over again?"

Holly shrugged. "I guess when you put it like that, yeah. Typically, I'm able to sense the attacks ahead of time. Divination is a big part of my power. Tarot cards, crystals, the whole shebang. I offer readings to people who are willing to listen. Most importantly, though, I'm a mother. Ever since my youngest started kindergarten, I've needed to find a new way to occupy my time while the kids are at school, so I've gone back to what I used to do, and that's giving readings."

"So Chris makes enough money to support the whole family?"

She nodded. "We have enough cash flow, yes. I help manage some of that, but we also hire someone to manage a big part of it, too. We've got a lot of rental properties and other investments. You know, passive forms of income." She rolled her eyes and shrugged. "Corporate stuff that neither of us really care for, but it's an essential part of living in this world."

Kathy *didn't* know. She was used to working low-paying jobs to make ends meet. Samantha was the one who knew all about investments and managing money and all of that. Without her, the girls never would've survived their father disappearing. Never would've been able to keep their family home. Without Samantha, this version of the future would've never happened.

But what Kathy could connect with Holly on was finding something to do during the day. Sure, Kathy watched Josh while Samantha and Steven were at work, and soon she'd have another little one to watch as well—and she loved her time with her nephew—but she couldn't help but feel like something was off. She had tried so many things to try to find her calling, but nothing had ever fit.

In a way, Kathy was envious of Holly for knowing who she was and finding a way to make that work for her. Then again, from what they had said about Future Kathy having "business" in New York, Kathy would eventually find her calling.

She debated asking Holly what that business was, specifically, but decided to let fate decide. Kathy would figure it out eventually. And she was content with allowing things to fall into place in the right time.

"So tell me more about these vampires," Kathy said. "How did it get so bad?"

"Well, clearly you know how it all started," Holly said.

"I know that part, but we're more than thirty years in the future and suddenly I feel like we're living in a dystopian world."

"There's times where that's certainly what it *feels* like, doesn't it?" Holly let out a heavy breath. "From what I understand, Aldric and Stockley have been gaining followers for years. Of course, we didn't know about any of that. Actually, *Detective* Dante Wilhelm was one of the first recruits." She rolled her eyes. "He's not even a real detective. The whole vampiric empire has been giving themselves titles to disarm people and make them believe that there's a sense of civility and order going on, when in reality the city has fallen into a military state."

Kathy thought of the empty neighborhoods and the loads of vampires coming out of the woodwork to capture them only hours before.

"At first it was a quiet change," Holly went on. "You noticed that the police chief looked paler. Then more of the police force began to look the same. Then they started acting erratically; people were being arrested and detained for stupid things. Speeding, littering, petty theft. Then when lawyers would try to fight the cases, then *they* started acting differently—and looking differently too. Before we knew it, there were more vampires in positions of power than people who *weren't* vampires. The whole police force, court systems, politicians, you name it. And not just in Erie, although this is where it started."

"How long has this been going on?"

"Chris and I started noticing these big changes over the last four or five years," Holly explained. "And then the absurd rules *for our safety* started being implemented. We couldn't ask someone if they were okay based purely on their skin tone. The whole 'see something, say something' idea went out the window.

Instead, we were encouraged to mind our own business. Oh, and the curfew! They've slowly been encroaching on more and more of our lives, all while they've been converting more and more people."

"Converting, as in making them vampires?"

Holly nodded. "There's hardly anyone left to fight it anymore. Anyone with any sense of authority has been turned. It's a war the Order of Magic would lose if we even tried to fight it."

"The Order of Magic?"

Holly shook her head. "Sorry. I think I've said too much already. The point is, the world is slowly becoming filled with vampires. Strong, charming, *dangerous* vampires. And immortal. They're not going away."

"Haven't you tried to kill any of them?"

"Sure we have, but we have two young kids. We need to make sure that *we* don't get implicated. They're literally *making up* charges just to get to people. I'm *not* going to do something stupid and be taken away from my children. I'm a mother before I'm a witch, as hard as that is for me sometimes."

Kathy studied Holly. She could tell that everything weighed heavy on her and, if Kathy were in those same shoes, she would feel the exact same stress and worry. But she also sensed that this was a test, a sign that the Fates wanted her to see, to know about the extent that one vampire bite extended to.

"Just how far is the vampiric reach?" Kathy asked.

The Fates

Holly was quiet for another few seconds, then she turned to Kathy. "I believe even the President of the United States is a vampire. He hasn't been doing public appearances and has signed bills perpetuating these insane rules that have already been implemented in Erie. This city is where the base of vampiric operations are, but I'm afraid Aldric and Stockley are about to take over the whole country."

"Wow." Kathy sat back against the couch. "So we really are on our own."

"We are. It's hard, especially knowing that this is the world I'm raising my children in. And each day, more and more vampires are created and joining the vampiric army. Their influence continues to grow. Soon they'll be unstoppable, if they're not already."

CHAPTER 16

The four of them reconvened in the foyer, where the altar was still spread out from when Chris and Holly had summoned Samantha and Kathy. The altar still had the silver candles in a circle, surrounding the oriental altar rug that was overlaid with herbs. On the table in the corner, incense still smoked, despite the stopper covering the air holes. Some things remained the same, no matter how far in the future they went.

"Are we ready?" Kathy asked with a heavy sigh as they faced each other. The sisters stood on one side of the altar while husband and wife stood on the other side.

Samantha didn't answer. She had a lump in her throat at the idea of leaving her adult son. At not getting the answers she so desperately wanted to know. Without getting a chance to see her grandchildren's faces.

But Chris was right. It was better for her not to know. It would all come in due time. She would meet them. She would help *shape* them. Eventually.

She had to be patient.

"Yeah, we should probably send you back," Holly said. "We want to prevent you from learning too much in the future and changing it, even by accident."

Chris nodded, although his eyes were locked with Samantha's.

Kathy knew that her sister wouldn't be the one to make the first move, so she started with the easiest goodbye: Holly.

"I can't thank you enough for showing us how bad things have gotten." What an unusual thing to thank someone for, but here they were. She stepped around the altar and gave Holly a hug. It was awkward and distant, but they both participated equally.

"You haven't seen the half of it," Holly said against Kathy's ear just before they pulled away.

"Trust me, we've seen enough," Kathy said. "I'm ready to go home and prevent all of this from occurring—well, the bad parts, anyway."

Holly sighed. "Not all the bad parts. Just the stupidity of this vampire rule. The good parts don't look so good when we don't have the bad parts to even them out." She shrugged. "But this is a bit too much bad for my liking."

"I agree," Kathy said with a chuckle.

They both turned to Samantha and Chris, who were still staring at each other over the altar. Finally, Samantha noticed the eyes on them, and stepped around the altar to her son.

She didn't even know where to begin. What did she say to her adult son who she hadn't even given birth to him yet? And how could she say goodbye after having only met him a few hours earlier?

She knew she had to go home. She knew it was the right thing to do. She knew she shouldn't ask too many questions. She knew that she didn't want to risk changing the makeup of her future family. Although, if what Samantha suspected was true and she wasn't around in this version of the future, she wanted to change that.

She was a ball of mixed emotions.

Without saying anything, she pulled Chris in for a tight hug. His arms quickly enveloped her and the two of them shed tears together.

Even though nobody was ever supposed to get a chance to meet their grown children, the time that Samantha had been given was not enough. She wanted more. She couldn't get enough of her kids.

When they did, eventually, pull away from one another, Samantha looked into his teary eyes—hers were wet as well—and said, "Magic truly is a special thing."

Chris simply smiled at her, and as his eyes crinkled from the smile, a few tears spilled from the corners and rolled down his cheeks.

Samantha reached up and wiped them away, then cupped his chin with her hand. "I've loved seeing what a great young man my little boy has become. And what a great father and husband, as well." She patted his cheek gently, then pulled her hand back. "Be safe."

"You too," he whispered. "I love you."

It was the first time one of her kids had told her he loved her. And she hadn't even expected it. And not who she expected to hear it from first. Her heart burst with love—and, at the same time, sorrow.

"I love you too. Forever and always."

Mother and son exchanged another emotional connection, wordlessly expressing their love for one another through their eyes.

Quietly, Holly clearly her throat. "Perhaps we should start the spell before Wilhelm and the rest of the vampires figure out where you are."

"What are you going to do if they attack after we've left?" Kathy asked.

Chris wiped at his eyes and looked down for a moment at the floor. When he looked back up, it was clear that he was avoiding eye contact with Samantha. "It doesn't matter what happens when you go. If the spell works like we want it to, you'll rewrite all of this. This exact same scenario will not ever repeat itself."

Samantha reached for Kathy's hand and they took their position in the center of the altar. She sniffled, then said, "Let's start the spell. Everybody ready?"

They nodded, then Holly pulled out her copy of the spell and shared it with Chris, while Kathy did the same with Samantha.

Channeling the Fates and our power,
Aid us now in this hour.
To correct the actions of the past,
And make changes that will surely last,
Send these witches back in time.
To fix this broken timeline.

After all four of them recited the spell, the air moved swiftly throughout the room before falling still again. And yet all four witches continued to look at one another unchanged.

"What happened?" Kathy asked, her eyes wide as she looked between the other three witches.

"It didn't work," Samantha said.

"Well, I *got* that, Sam!" Kathy blurted. "Why not?"

"Maybe—"

The front doors burst open and in walked Detective Dante Wilhelm along with other vampires. From the kitchen, more vampires swarmed in. The witches turned to the sunroom, but even that had vampires blocking the way.

They were surrounded.

CHAPTER 17

Holly darted for the stairs, but stopped when her worst fears were realized: two vampires came down the stairs, each of them holding one of her children, both of whom were screaming. Her oldest, Sophia, was kicking and punching and doing her best to try to break free from her captor, but the vampire's strength was too strong.

"Put them down!" Holly demanded. She reached for the closest vampire, trying to pry his arm off of her son, but another one, who had emerged from the back door, met her on the steps and pulled her back.

"Hands off, witch!"

"Please don't make things worse for yourself by resisting arrest," Wilhelm said from the front door.

THE FATES

"You bastard!" Chris charged toward the so-called detective. Within seconds, his fists were surrounded by magical flame. As he raised his arms to the intruders, the flame shot in a line out toward Wilhelm.

Two vampires jumped in the line of fire, taking the hit. They let out cries of agony and then burst into flames without a trace left behind.

Brandishing his flame again, Chris fired another attack at Wilhelm, who stepped into the living room, out of sight from Chris. Meanwhile, two more vampires by the door took the hit and burst into flames.

At the sign of attack, the rest of the vampires moved in to restrain the witches, which resulted in an all-out brawl.

Kathy froze as many vampires as she could, while Samantha rushed to Holly's aid to help with the kids. Despite Kathy's power having taken effect, more vampires rushed in behind them, bumping into the frozen ones and breaking the effect of her power.

They moved in, cornering Kathy against a wall. Her eyes darted toward Samantha and Holly, who weren't having any better luck at fighting off the vampires near the stairs. And Chris's magical flames erupting near the front door had died down as well.

They were completely outnumbered and their powers were no match. Now Kathy could see why the vampires hadn't been stopped before. Once they had gained strength in numbers, nobody stood a chance. Especially the nonmagical.

And yet, oddly, none of the vampires were trying to bite them. They needed them to be free thinkers as witches. Not mindless loyal zombie followers. They needed something from the witches, meaning that they weren't going to turn them. Not yet, at least.

One-by-one the witches were each restrained and brought together in a line. Each of them had their hands held tightly behind their backs.

Sophia had stopped crying, although the terror was very evident in her eyes. She was trying to put on a brave face in front of the vampires.

Her little brother, however, was a different story. He was in hysterics, crying and screaming and fighting to get away from the vampire holding him. His squirms became too much and a second vampire had to come to assist with the restraint.

"Shut that kid up or get him out of here," Wilhelm demanded as he emerged from the safety of the living room, now that the witches had been restrained. "And take the older one, too, while you're at it."

The vampires complied with his demands and carried the kids out through the front door.

"No!" Holly cried as she watched her children disappear into the night. "If you hurt them, I *swear* I will find a way to kill you! Even if I have to come back from the dead to do it!"

Wilhelm laughed. "That fight in you will come in handy,

once I make you part of the Vampiric Empire."

With no other options, Holly spit at him. Even though he had started to turn away, it had landed on his shoulder. He looked at the spot on him, then glanced at Holly with hatred in his eyes.

After a few tense seconds, he wiped his shoulder clean before stepping toward each of the witches. He hissed at them, and every witch flinched back involuntarily. All except Samantha.

Wilhelm laughed to himself again and stepped up to Samantha. "You must be a special kind of stupid, breaking out of a vampire prison after revealing you're a witch."

Their eyes locked, remaining heated as they sized each other up. Samantha was not going to let him intimidate her, no matter if she was restrained. Maybe it was her mind specialty, or maybe it was the attack on her family, but she remained fully in control of her emotions, despite embracing them only moments before the vampires had rushed in.

"Every witch is required to register with the Empire," Wilhelm went on. "Your name, address, and a full list of your magical abilities, in full detail. We also collect the names of your family members to make sure that everyone you're related to is documented as well."

Samantha narrowed her eyes. This was part of the future that she hadn't known before. As she learned more and more about this vampiric future, the more it reminded her of the horror stories she had learned in history class. The ones they were taught to try to prevent the unimaginable from happening again.

Clearly, they had failed.

"And yet," Wilhelm went on, "you are nowhere in our system. Why is that?"

Samantha made sure she had a mental guard up, in case there was a witch-turned-vampire in their midst who shared the same abilities as her. She couldn't give up any of their secrets, even accidentally. "You said it yourself. I'm special."

Wilhelm raised his eyebrows, not at all fazed by her bravery. "Really? You are still refusing to say anything, even if it would save your family?"

Samantha couldn't keep the surprise from her face. How did Wilhelm find out that she and Chris were family? She had only given him her first name, but he had used some advanced technology to scan her face to look for the records in their system when she and Kathy had first been arrested. But that hadn't resulted in any search results, from what she understood.

Unless he was lying. Maybe Wilhelm knew more than he led on and—

No. He had found a record for *Kathy*, but not for Samantha. Which meant that he could find Samantha's record through Kathy.

But he wasn't questioning Kathy at the moment. He was questioning Samantha. Asking her why *she* didn't have a record in their system, which implied that Kathy *did* have one. And if Samantha didn't have one, then that meant—

"Take them away," Wilhelm told his crew. "Back to the prison, where they belong. Maybe after we start to tear apart the family, we'll finally get some answers."

"No!" Holly cried. "Don't hurt my babies! They didn't do anything!"

"You son of a bitch!" Chris hollered. "I'll kill you! I'll rip you apart and kill you! You bastard!"

Amidst the chaos, Samantha kept her eyes on Wilhelm, even as the vampires started to drag her away. She couldn't believe how powerless she felt. She couldn't believe that nobody would come to their defense. She couldn't believe any of this was happening. It was so far beyond her scope of reality.

And yet it was her reality. Before long, she was being dragged down the street as a prisoner, and as she looked desperately to the neighbors for help, all she saw were closed curtains and dark porches.

They were on their own.

CHAPTER 18

Detective Dante Wilhelm came into the interrogation room and slammed the door behind him, startling Samantha in her seat. She was handcuffed to a bar in the center of the table.

He leaned over the table, in an effort to intimidate the witch. And although his skin was white and she could see the thirst for her blood in his eyes, she returned his scowl.

"I'm going to give you one last chance to give me some answers," he demanded. "Where did you come from and why are you here?"

Samantha wanted to sit back and cross her arms. Show Wilhelm that he was not going to scare her into giving up her secrets. But her hands were chained to the table, so she simply interlaced her fingers, trying to appear as unbothered as possible, and looked up at him without saying a word.

Wilhelm held her stare for a while, then slammed the table hard and came around to her side. In one swift motion, he grabbed a fistful of her hair and jerked her head back.

"You might think you're so tough because you and your sister managed to escape from our prison, but don't forget that *I* have the upper hand here. One bite could kill you or turn you."

Either way, Samantha knew that she was dead, if Wilhelm had it his way. So she kept quiet. Even though she could feel him ripping hair from her scalp, she remained strong, thinking about her adult son and his wife in agony over having their children removed. The cries of those children as they were pulled from their beds and hauled away from their home after having done nothing wrong fueled Samantha's veins with anger and hatred toward the vampires. Specifically, Wilhelm, who had ordered the removal.

Wilhelm released her and began to pace around the room. "You know, the funny thing is, we found a record for Kathy in our database. But, as I've already told you, there is no record for you. Do you have any idea why that is?"

Samantha's hard stare softened, only slightly. This reveal from Wilhelm confirmed her suspicions: Samantha was dead in this world. The record they found for Kathy *had* to be future Kathy.

So how young had Samantha died? If they were only thirty

years in the future, she should be fifty-five. She should still have plenty of life left in her. So much more of her family to enjoy.

Except, she wouldn't. And that's what Chris had refused to tell her.

Samantha felt unsettled by that fact. She wanted to be able to see her children grow up. She wanted to be able to meet her grandchildren. She wanted to live life to the fullest. And yet, somehow, she was going to miss out on all of that.

When did her life fall apart?

Wilhelm slapped her hard across the face. "Where are you from?"

The rage built up inside of Samantha. The disappointment. The sadness. All of it channeled into hatred for the vampires. Jutting out her jaw, she stared daggers at him and snarled, "Go to hell."

That ignited the vampire instincts in Wilhelm. He peeled back his lips and flashed his fangs. A menacing hiss escaped his throat and he lunged at her viable throat with his teeth.

This is it, she thought. *This is how I go.*

But then another thought came to her: she was pregnant with Chris. And he was perfectly healthy in this time. So that meant that Wilhelm *couldn't* kill her—or turn her. Not while she was still pregnant. That would immediately change the course of the future and launch them into a time paradox. The Fates wouldn't allow that.

Unless the Fates were no longer watching.

THE FATES

The door to the interrogation room opened suddenly and Wilhelm snapped his attention to the door. Another vampire had stepped in and stopped when he saw how close Wilhelm had come to biting Samantha. There was a tense silence that followed for a few seconds before Wilhelm recovered.

"What do you want?" he demanded. He took a step away from Samantha and began pacing the room again. Embarrassment for having briefly lost control evident on his face.

"Uh…the, uh, the sister didn't tell us anything," the vampire at the door said.

Wilhelm ground his teeth and looked at Samantha through the mirror on the wall. She could see the look of disgust in his eyes. The fact that she wasn't intimidated by him and had pushed him to a point he thought he had overcome—an instinct he thought he had control over—had clearly set him off.

And that made Samantha quite satisfied.

Finally, Wilhelm turned to the vampire at the door. "Take this one back to her cell. Maybe these witches will talk after they've had time to grow tired and hungry." Before exiting the room, he turned back to Samantha and added, "And think about the pain we can inflict on the children."

Samantha was grateful that he turned suddenly and left the room. Otherwise, he would've seen her stern exterior crack with worry.

CHAPTER 19

Kathy was tossed into the prison cell hard. She put out her hands to catch herself, feeling the rough concrete floor scrape at her palms at the impact. By the time she turned around, the prison door slammed shut with a click that signaled it locking.

She got to her feet and pressed herself against the bars. "You can lock me up all you want!" she called to the guard down the corridor. "I'm still not going to talk! You're going to have to turn me if you want to know what I know!"

"Don't push them," a quiet voice said.

Kathy looked around, confused at who was talking. The woman in the cell across from her was asleep on her cot, unfazed by Kathy's outburst. Yet the voice sounded like it was coming from somewhere close.

"Hello?" she asked.

"I'm right next to you," the voice said again. A woman's voice. Small. Tired. Kind.

Kathy followed the sound of the voice. She pressed her back against the brick wall separating their cells. "What's your name?"

"Riley," she said. "You're Kathy?"

She nodded, then realized that Riley couldn't see her, so added, "Yeah. How did you know?"

"They're pretty pissed about you," she said. "The guards, that is. All the prisoners are very happy for you and your sister. We just wish you could've saved us all."

"Us too. We're working on, though."

"Be careful," Riley warned.

"I'm not afraid of them."

"You should be. At least a little bit. Becoming a vampire has ripped out their humanity. They don't care that they're killing people, splitting up families, causing unspeakable grief. But they will use it to their advantage. They know that we have souls, and that we care for one another. And they'll exploit that."

Kathy sighed. She could hear the pain in Riley's voice. The complete sense of loss she must've felt at the hands of the vampires. "You sound like you're speaking from personal experience."

"I am. I used to be one of those people who refused to believe that things had gotten so bad. I figured all of this talk was just conspiracy theories. That the systems we had put in place would hold up in the face of such gross injustice. But I was wrong."

"What happened?" Kathy pushed. She had no immediate way of getting out of the prison cell, so she needed to gain as much information and insight as possible. If the Fates were still paying attention, the more Kathy knew, the sooner she could go back to her time and correct all of this from happening.

It was the last bit of hope she had to hold on to, now that she knew magic wouldn't be able to send them back to their time.

Besides that, she was genuinely curious how people had let things get so bad.

"Two months ago, a bunch of my girlfriends and I went on a wine weekend up near North East and into the Southern Tier of New York. We were only gone one night, but when I came back I noticed that things were…different."

"Different how?"

"Just small things, at first. My kids didn't run to greet me with hugs and kisses when I came home. My husband barely looked at me. I wrote it off as them having a bad day, or being distracted by other things, or me not being gone that long. But, if I'm being honest, I knew that something was off about them right away. I didn't want to believe it. They were my family. They were the ones I loved. The ones I devoted my life to." She took in another deep breath that had a shaky exhale. "Later that night, I questioned my husband when we were alone. He tried to reassure me that everything was fine, but I knew it wasn't. So I kept pushing and pushing." She broke off as the tears overcame her.

"He had been turned?"

Riley sniffled. "Yes. He finally admitted it, saying that they *cleansed* him—and the kids, too. Then he forced me into the car and drove me to the Infirmary."

"He forced you? How?"

"He told me it was the best way to keep an open mind about the future. I didn't want to go—it was late and the kids were in bed. At least, I thought they were. When he finally showed me that they were out doing night patrols with the rest of them, that's when it finally sunk in."

They were quiet as Kathy remembered the terror on the faces of Chris and Holly's kids. It turned her stomach that this was happening to innocent children. But Riley was right, becoming a vampire ripped out any trace of humanity.

"What's the Infirmary?" Kathy asked after a few quiet moments.

"It's where they turn people. Trick them into thinking it's a spa weekend or something. Whatever excuse they come up with when they're trying to convert people of their own accord. But because I was still skeptical, they said they needed more time to decide, claiming that there was a waiting list. As if people *wanted* to be turned."

"But if they have so many vampires now, can't anyone turn people into vampires?"

"No. There's only a select few who are approved to turn others into vampires. That way, the mind control remains intact."

"Hence, the waiting list." Kathy looked at her nails, focusing on something so minuscule and unimportant when the gravity of her situation threatened to consume her mind.

"I'm on the list to be converted," Riley said through her tears. "And honestly? I don't even care. I've already lost my family. My kids…the look in their eyes wasn't theirs. Their touch was so cold. Lifeless, really. There was no love in their eyes. And the fact that they were out patrolling like soldiers tells me that there's nothing left in them. My kids are dead, even if their bodies are still walking around. Same with my husband. I may as well be too."

"Riley, I know this might sound too good to be true," Kathy started. "It may even sound impossible, but I promise you, one way or another, I will find a way to stop all of this and prevent it from ever happening. I just need to find a way out."

Riley let out a dark chuckle. "There is no way out. This is the end of the world. The end of my life. I've lost everything."

The Fates

Kathy didn't say anything in response to that. The woman was in mourning. No amount of reassurance from a stranger would change the facts of her life.

But Kathy had hope. After all, she had found a way to break out of the prison before. She could do it again. She had to.

CHAPTER 20

Unlike Kathy, Samantha had no one to talk to in her prison cell. With the late hour, everyone around her seemed to be sleeping—not that she could see anyone other than the prisoner in the cell directly across from her who was, in fact, sleeping beneath a thin threadbare blanket.

Samantha paced her cell as she contemplated her options. They needed to escape—again. But breaking out of a vampire prison once was a long shot, to do it a second time in the same *day* would be impossible. Security would be heightened. Samantha and her sister, specifically, would be watched extra closely.

If Samantha couldn't escape herself, maybe she could try to help from the confines of her cell. After all, her specialty was the mind, and she could see if she could stretch that to other parts of the prison. Places where Chris and Holly's kids might be hidden.

Samantha's grandchildren.

That thought was staggering to her, the fact that she was a grandmother in this time. Especially to a child that she hadn't even given birth to yet.

She touched her hand to her belly absently and looked out down the hall. Would she be held captive for months? Would she give birth in this prison cell, away from the comforts of home—the comforts of her time? Away from her husband and older son. Would they need to find a way to transport mother and baby back to their appropriate time? Was that even possible? And what kind of long-term effect would that have on her, Chris, and the timeline?

Taking a seat back on the cot in her cell, she leaned back against the cinderblocks and brought her feet up under her.

Her thoughts traveled to Josh, back in 1991, having no idea that his mother was trapped in a prison in the future. If she didn't make it home to him, he would think she abandoned him.

Much like Samantha's father abandoned her and Kathy. Or maybe he had found himself in a magical mess similar to this one.

Shaking her head, she forced herself to focus on the positives. Chris knew who she was in this time. And he lived in their ancestral home, which meant that Samantha *had* to have made it back home to her time so that she could raise both Josh and Chris.

And what a well-adjusted man Chris turned out to be. Was that due to her parenting? Or did someone else raise him in her absence? What Detective Wilhelm had alluded to was the fact that Samantha was not alive in this future.

Samantha tried to pass it off as Wilhelm lying in order to get her to talk, but a memory in her head persisted: Chris had alluded to the same thing. And what benefit would it be to him to lie to her? Not to mention, the pain in his eyes when he saw his mother alive and well was genuine.

So there was truth in there somewhere.

Just as Samantha felt the sadness begin to take over, she shoved it back down. She had to remind herself of one thing: according to the Fates, this version of the future was only one possibility. There was still time to change it.

That made Samantha feel better. There was so much about this future that she wanted to change.

CHAPTER 21

The guards stopped magically in their tracks as they passed by Kathy's cell. This time, the one guard was close enough that she had no trouble snatching his keys from his belt and freeing herself—yet again—from her confines.

But the moment she slid open the cell bars, a blaring alarm started that set Kathy into motion.

Darting past the frozen guards, she raced down the cell block. Her head was on a swivel, looking back and forth in search of Samantha's cell. She figured her sister would've reached out to her telepathically if she saw that the guards were somewhere close, so that must've meant that Samantha wasn't on the same level as her. It was no surprise, really, considering their previous prison break.

At the end of the block was a metal door that she knew led out to the staircase. Just as she burst through it, she collided with a vampire on the other side, who quickly wrapped his arms around her to restrain her.

Kathy flailed in his hold, then used the tight confines of the stairwell to her advantage. Using the wall as leverage, she pedaled her feet up the cinder blocks and spun as the vampire's hold on her inevitably loosened.

She narrowly missed falling down the stairs from the top of the platform, catching herself only on the metal handrail that had been installed to prevent that very such thing. Spinning around, she froze the vampire guard, then did the same to the other two racing up the stairs below her.

With no time to catch her breath, she sprinted down the stairs and had to quickly freeze another guard as he came into the stairwell.

Despite the multiple freezes, the alarm sirens continued to blare loudly throughout the prison, rousing prisoners and bringing in more and more vampires from the other end of the cell block.

Kathy raced down the lower level cell block and found her sister's cell, where Samantha stood near the bars, looking up and down the corridor.

"I knew it was you," she said.

"Yeah, who else would be this crazy to break out of this hellhole twice?" Kathy fumbled with the keys she had snatched from the guard, trying to find the right one for Samantha's lock.

"Look out!" Samantha shouted.

Kathy looked up just in time to see a vampire hissing at her from behind. She jumped out of the way, then turned and froze him in place. With the way that he magically stopped moving, she had to duck under the vampire to get to the lock on Samantha's cell.

Finally, the door slid opened with a loud *clink* and the sisters forced it open. Warily, Samantha stepped through into the corridor, again ducking under the frozen menacing gaze of the vampire.

"We need to get out of here and get in touch with the Fates," Kathy said. "Should we try the garbage chute again?"

Samantha shook her head. "No. They'll be expecting that. We have to find a different way. But before we do that, we need to find Chris and Holly and the kids. Have you seen them anywhere?"

"No. They must have them somewhere else. Are you sure you want to take the time for them?" Kathy asked. If they were successful and the timeline was reset, then the kids wouldn't ever be in danger in the first place.

Before Samantha could answer, a door down the corridor slammed open and they heard more vampire hisses echo throughout the concrete hallway.

"Our window of opportunity to escape is small enough as it is," Kathy said. "And if we get back to our time, all of this will be rewritten anyway."

"I can't leave them, no matter what happens with the timeline," Samantha said. "They're my family. I can't turn my back on them."

The door at the end of the corridor opened, leaving Kathy no time to argue. She grabbed Samantha's hand and raced directly toward the incoming vampires. She waited until they were closer, then put up her hand and froze them in place.

The sisters dashed toward the end of the cell block, where the vampires stood frozen. They needed to sneak through before any others tried to interfere. And from there, Kathy had no idea where they were going to hide.

"I searched upstairs and down here and didn't see Chris, Holly, and the kids," Kathy said as they ran.

"Then they have to be somewhere else."

They came to the vampires at the end and stopped. Kathy went first, carefully stepping around them, so as not to bump into them and accidentally unfreeze them. It was like picking her way through a myriad of lasers, the way she needed to bend and twist her body around the frozen vamps.

"They must be in an interrogation room," Samantha went on. "Do you remember how to get back to the one they put you in?"

"Sure, but I doubt that's the only one they have." Kathy straightened, finding herself in the middle of three other vampires. She eyed up her next move, crouched down to get a better angle, and stepped around them. "You saw this place from the outside. It's huge."

Samantha sighed. "Yeah. Do you think there's any chance that I can sense for them? See if I can pick up on any of their thoughts?"

"You tell me." Kathy picked her way to the other side, then waved her sister on once she was cleared. "You would know better, but I think that such a populated place like this would be hard to hear the thoughts of the ones you're trying to find."

The older sister was quiet. She followed Kathy's steps, picking her way around the frozen vampires. "Well, we need to find them. I'm not giving up on them. They have to be here somewhere."

Once they were both past the frozen vampires, they turned to the door and opened it slowly. The alarm sirens were still blaring, but in the hallway just outside of the cell blocks, there were red lights flashing as well, which only added to the chaos.

Kathy peered through the small glass window at the top of the door and, upon seeing the coast was clear, turned the handle and exited the cell block.

On the other side, there were two doors opposite each other, leading to hallways where the rest of the prison staff were housed.

"Which one do you think we should choose?" Kathy asked her sister.

"I don't know. I'm trying to search for their thoughts but—" Samantha stopped cold.

When Kathy turned to see what it was that she noticed, she saw it for herself: two imposing vampires emerging from the shadows. The worst part was that Kathy had seen them before. The one was the man that they had failed to save back in their time. And the other was the vampire who had bitten him.

Aldric and Stockley.

Quickly, more vampires began piling into the space. The sirens and flashing lights cut out.

"This was a trap," Samantha said.

Aldric smiled. "And you fell right into it."

CHAPTER 22

"What do you want from us?" Samantha asked. She kept her back turned only to Kathy and, intuitively, the sisters turned in sync together so that their backs were never exposed to any of the vampires that surrounded them, and were hissing at them.

"You know, we both remember you girls from that night over thirty years ago," Aldric said. "Granted, I remember it better than Stockley. That was his rebirth, so everything was still new for him."

"It's when my life truly began," Stockley added.

"You both were there that night," Aldric went on. "You tried to stop me from converting Stockley and giving him a new life."

"You failed," Stockley added for emphasis.

"We can't have a perfect record all the time," Kathy said. "I mean, look at you. We've broken out of your prison twice now."

"Only once," Aldric said with a smirk. "You haven't left the facility this time. But I digress. The point is, you two were there the night our rule over the world truly began."

Don't let them know that we've time traveled, Samantha warned her sister telepathically. *Even if the Fates were the ones to help us. Fates change all the time through free will, and maybe this was a circumstance they didn't foresee.*

So what if they know? Kathy thought to herself, which Samantha read with ease.

If the possibility of time travel suddenly becomes a reality, the vampires may find a way to access time travel themselves to protect that pivotal moment in time, rendering it impossible for us to correct our mistake.

Oh, Kathy thought simply. *Good point.*

"What's your point?" Kathy asked out loud. "Why is it so important for you to keep us captive? Is it because you're afraid of us? Afraid we'll talk and spread a rebellion?"

Don't provoke him, Samantha warned.

Aldric and Stockley both looked at each other, then burst into laughter. Soon, the rest of the room followed suit as well. All except the sisters.

The growing humor in what Samantha viewed as a humorless situation made her uneasy. She resisted the urge to ask for more clarity. That would only make the vampires believe her and Kathy to be stupid.

"It's more a matter of what you want from us," Aldric said. "After all, I know that something isn't right."

"We could sense it the moment you came into the prison," Stockley said.

"Not right?" Kathy asked. "Not right, how?"

"You see, unlike vampires, witches *age*," Stockley went on. "And, it appears, that you haven't aged a day since we last saw each other."

"A curious thing, isn't it?" Aldric added.

Samantha saw a hunger in Aldric's eyes. Then, as she looked around the room, she saw the same look in all of the vampires' eyes. Absently, she reached for her sister's hand. They would need to rely on each other if they were to survive this.

Aldric stepped closer—so close that Samantha could almost feel the chill of his skin, as if it were radiating off his body. Or rather, sucking the life from hers. "I've seen a lot in my years," he said. "I've had so many of them. So many lives have passed before my eyes—certainly, I have rebirthed so many more. And yet, this particular circumstance is a quandary to me. Tell me, where did you come from? Because, surely, you are not like any of the others that I have come to reign over. You are not of this world. So which one do you belong to?"

Samantha held his stare, despite the fact that his intimidation tactics were getting to her. His imposing, large frame as it towered over her, sucking the heat off her body like it craved it. And yet, he seemed to have a persuasion of his own, that was almost stronger than the one that Samantha wielded herself. She was usually impenetrable from those kinds of manipulation methods, but she felt herself *wanting* to tell him what she had just told Kathy to keep quiet about.

Behind Aldric, there was movement as the crowd of vampires moved out of the way for someone coming into the tight space.

"Sir," Wilhelm said as he broke through the crowd. He addressed Aldric, but nodded in Stockley's direction as he stepped by him. "The other witches have escaped."

Yes! Samantha proclaimed in her head, focusing all of the rest of her energy on keeping her face stoic amidst Aldric's scrutiny.

The vampire turned to Wilhelm. "They've *escaped*? How is that possible?"

Samantha felt a tug on her arm. Kathy subtly nodded to the hallway in the opposite direction. Samantha took one quick look around, saw that the vampires were distracted, then followed her sister's lead and broke through the crowd, dashing for the hallway in the corner.

They felt hands reaching for them, but none of the grasps made purchase. It wasn't until Samantha and Kathy heard the doors slam shut behind them that Samantha felt just how much her heart had been racing.

CHAPTER 23

They dashed through the hallway. Several times, heads popped out of doorways. Each time, Kathy froze them, trying to prevent anyone else from following them. There was no telling who was a vampire and who was an innocent human just trying to survive under the vampiric rule.

At the end of the hall, the doors opened to another landing with more hallways off of it. This one seemed friendlier. The walls were painted a calming neutral color, plush chairs filled a waiting area, clean carpets covered the floors and made the room seem quieter and calmer. Tucked in the corner were vending machines and beside that was a drinking fountain and bathrooms. It was as if this area was intended to be seen by people who *weren't* prisoners.

That meant they were getting closer to the exit.

"What is this place?" Kathy asked as she looked around.

"Maybe the base of operations for the Vampiric Empire," Samantha suggested. "Or maybe this is just to make people feel like their loved ones *aren't* imprisoned."

There was a crash down the hall from where they had come and the girls moved quickly around the corner and out of sight from the windows in the doors.

They huddled near the vending machines and sized up the doorways around them. None of them had windows or name cards on the walls beside them, making it impossible to tell where each door led. They didn't have time to open each one and investigate for themselves.

"What do we do now?" Kathy asked.

Samantha shrugged. "We have to find a way out of here."

"But we've never been in this part of the building before," Kathy said. "We have no idea where to go!"

"Well, if the kids are being held somewhere other than the prison, it has to be somewhere soundproof. Somewhere away from areas like this."

"Like someone's office? Do vampires even *have* offices?"

"If they're trying to keep up appearances, they do," Samantha said. "And those private areas would probably require a keycard, or some other form of entry that limits the number of people who can access it."

Kathy looked around the room. She pointed at a door that

had a small, flat gray panel beside the doorknob. "There!"

Samantha followed her sister's finger and approached the door. "Exactly." She tugged on the handle but, just as she expected, it didn't budge. "The question is, how do we get in?"

"A spell?"

"I think the vampires would've prepared for that. My guess is that they have witches on staff."

"They still use physical keys for the prison cells," Kathy pointed out. "So it's worth a shot to try."

Before Samantha could reply, though, they heard a crash from a door off of the waiting area.

Both girls quickly ran for cover, finding a spot in between the vending machines. They huddled together and waited, Kathy on the outside of the tight space, in case she needed to freeze whatever attacker might come up on them. The bright side was that the crash came from another room. The threat wasn't immediate, even if it was imminent.

"Should we try to make a run for it?" Kathy asked in a whisper over her shoulder.

"To where?" Samantha replied from behind her. "We have no idea where these doors lead and, for all we know, they could all be locked."

Another crash—an explosion, really—and closer this time.

"So, what? Are we just supposed to sit here and wait for them to come to us?"

"If we have any hope of getting a key to that door, we need

them to follow us," Samantha said. "Aldric and Stockley are sure to have a key. Hell, I'm sure Wilhelm does too. If they follow us, you can freeze them, then steal the key and get in."

"*If* they freeze," Kathy murmured.

Another explosion. This time through one of the doors in the office area where they had been a few minutes ago. The girls hushed their voices, then crouched down in the tight space, trying to make themselves as small as possible.

Kathy forced her breathing to slow, even though her heart rattled in her chest. She listened carefully for where the intruder might be, or how many of them there were. But she couldn't hear anything.

The explosion hadn't been loud enough to make her ears ring, but she found it odd that she couldn't hear a sound. Was it a spell that made her go deaf, to cloak her attacker's advances?

No. She still heard the quiet murmur of the HVAC system blowing air into the space, and the humming of the vending machine beside her.

Do you think the coast is clear? Samantha pinged into her head.

Glancing over her shoulder, Kathy shrugged, then quickly turned her eyes back to her front. She couldn't see beyond the vending machine, and considered taking a step out until she saw a shadow move in the space in front of her.

The carpet kept the footsteps silent.

She put her hands up, getting ready to freeze.

The Fates

Another step and a boot came into view, followed by the rest of the man.

Chris, with Holly by his side.

CHAPTER 24

Samantha let out a breath of relief at the sight of Chris and Holly.

"Are you guys okay?" Chris asked, beating Samantha to the punch.

"We're fine." Kathy stood and extracted herself from their crude hiding place.

"What about you guys?" Samantha asked.

"Physically, we're fine," Holly said. "Have you guys seen Sophia and Griffin?"

Samantha shook her head. "No. That's who we were looking for. We think they might be hidden in someone's office, or somewhere else away from the rest of the prisoners."

"Any idea where?" Chris asked.

THE FATES

Kathy pointed to the door with the keypad. "Possibly through there, depending on where that leads."

"It's locked, so we think it might lead to a private office, or a hallway to a private office, or something," Samantha clarified.

"We can't waste our time going through doors *hoping* to find the right one," Holly said with a frustrated groan. "We have to find them before they move them—or hurt them."

"Should we try a location ritual?" Kathy suggested.

Nobody had a chance to debate her idea. The door that Samantha and Kathy had come through suddenly burst open, flying right off the hinges and dropping to the floor.

Chris turned to the door with the keypad and, with a swift gesture of his hands, the solid wood door blew into kindling that scattered all over the floor.

This time, Samantha felt the ringing in her ears. But she didn't need to hear to be able to see Chris run through the door and the rest of their ragtag group follow.

The opposite side of the door led to a cozier office setting. There were cubicles, where workers remained—surprised to find prisoners walking among them. Many of them ducked under their desks for cover. One brave man charged after Chris with a chair over his head.

Chris caught the chair before it made contact, broke it free of the man's grip, and pushed it aside, then kicked the man in the stomach.

"Chris!" Samantha scolded. "You don't have to be as cruel as them!"

Her son paid her no mind as he raced around the cubicles to several offices lining the outer walls. Chris peered through the windows of each office before settling on one nestled in an alcove. One that led to an office inside another office.

Behind them, the vampires were gaining on them, splitting into different directions and quickly floating toward them, many of them hissing with bloodlust.

Chris tried the door and it was unlocked. The four witches filed in quickly and Kathy locked the door behind them.

Inside the office, there was a terrified older woman. To Samantha's surprise, her complexion was warmer than the vampires they had been escaping from. Did they have civilians working for them alongside the vampires? They had innocent people aiding in these horrors?

Chris and Holly didn't seem to notice the skin color. He picked up the woman by her shirt and brought her to his face.

"Where are they?" he growled.

"Who? Who are you looking for?" The woman began to cry. "Please! Please don't hurt me!"

"Ours kids!" Holly added. "They took them! The bastards took them! Where are they keeping them?"

"I don't know! Truly, I don't! I would tell you if I knew!"

Chris raised his fist and it burst into flame, ready to strike.

"Who do you work for?" Kathy blurted. Her hand naturally

went to Chris's arm and she tried to push his firy hand away from the terrified woman. "Whose office is this?"

"D-Director of L-Licensing, J-Janie Pearl," she stammered.

"What does that mean?" Samantha asked.

"We register every resident. Name, age, race, magical status."

"This is where you keep track of witches?" Samantha asked.

The woman nodded. "Among other creatures, yes."

Creatures. In this reality, they weren't even dignified with humanity.

On the other side of the door, they heard fists pounding and more hisses. Chris, growing agitated, slammed the woman against the wall.

"Where would they be keeping the kids? You know this office better than we do! And *don't* lie to me!"

Tears fell from the woman's eyes as she began to get more hysterical. She sobbed and used her feet to kick under her, trying to get purchase on any surface she could to extract herself from Chris's hold.

"Chris," Samantha said under her breath. She didn't want him to hurt the woman, but she also understood his desperation to find his children.

"Th-There's a gun room off of D-Dante's office," she said. "I don't *know* that they're—that they're—that they're *there*, but i-if he was h-hiding them, that's where I th-think they'd b-be."

Chris's fire magic extinguished as he dropped her to the

floor and stepped away from her to pace the room. The pounding fists on the door beat louder.

"Dante?" Kathy asked.

"Wilhelm," Holly clarified, then turned to the woman. "Where is his office?"

The woman pointed through the door. "Out there. Straight down that row of cubicles. His n-name is on the d-door."

Samantha turned to the door. "We'd have to go back out there."

"Then that's what we're going to do." Chris marched past his mother and to the door.

"Chris…" Holly seemed to hesitate too. "I'm with you on this. I'd walk through fire to get our kids back, but we can't be stupid and get ourselves killed. We need a game plan. Otherwise we're dead—and then the fangs have our kids anyway."

He ground his teeth together. "Fine. You want a plan? I open the door and hit them with as much fire as I can. Those suckers hate fire. They'll either die or run off. Aunt Kathy, you freeze the stragglers. Sounds good?"

"Well, actually—" Samantha started, but Chris swung the door open without hearing her out.

The vampires swarmed in the doorway, but Chris extended both hands and shot fire from his palms.

It was now or never.

CHAPTER 25

The vampires howled as they were incinerated with Chris's magical flames. He stepped out through the doorway, pushing back the remaining vampires into the cubicle office space, pushing them back enough for the women to escape out of the room behind him.

Kathy searched the space for stragglers. Anyone who might be going to get reinforcements. There were two, and she froze them before they could flee through the door.

Then, turning, she saw the remaining vampires lunging at Chris, trying to bite him, but backing off when he wielded flames with his fists. She put up her hands and froze them before they could hurt her nephew.

Samantha and Holly ran to the door the woman in the office

had indicated. Outside, there was a placard that said, DETECTIVE DANTE WILHELM.

The door opened easily and they stepped inside, which was a stark contrast from the explosions and commotion out in the outer office area.

Like the room where they had questioned the woman, this office space had a secretary area with several doors off of it.

"Which room is it?" Samantha asked.

"Only one way to find out." Holly went to the first door and opened it. A conference room.

Kathy braced herself against the main door and was soon joined by Chris. After a minute, he moved to push the closest desk in front of the door to better serve as a barricade, since they didn't have a key to the door.

"We'll need to find another way out once we find the kids," Chris said when he was sure the door was secure.

"If the kids are even in here." Holly opened another door to yet another empty office.

The room on the other side of Samantha's door led to the viewing room into the interrogation room, which had another exit that, for now, seemed quiet on the other side. "I may have found a possible way to escape."

"Or a way for more vamps to get in." Kathy came up beside her sister and peered inside. She remembered the harsh interrogation she faced earlier.

"My question is, why is it so empty?" Samantha asked.

"Maybe they've fled to safety," Chris said as he inspected the space, opening desk drawers and examining documents left out. "Or maybe they're trying to lure us into a trap."

Holly nodded. "I sense that the kids are nearby."

Samantha nodded. "Me too. We're getting close."

"But where are they?" Kathy asked.

"We'll find them," Chris said. "Even if I have to tear this whole place apart with my bare hands."

Holly furrowed her brow and looked to Samantha. "Are you picking up on that feeling too?"

Samantha closed her eyes and focused. Her sensing abilities weren't the strength of her specialty, but more a byproduct of it. But she focused and, finally, she locked on to that feeling that Holly had been picking up on too. "Danger."

"Well yeah." Kathy gestured to the door, where the vampires were beating on it from the other side. "That much is obvious."

Holly shook her head. "No, not that. There's another danger. Something we haven't discovered yet."

"The kids?" Samantha asked.

"I think so," Holly said. "They're protected."

"As we suspected," Chris said. "But where?"

Suddenly, as if they were all in sync, their attention collectively focused on the one remaining door that they hadn't passed through yet.

"Could it be that easy?" Kathy asked.

"Only one way to find out." Chris started to the door, but

paused when he heard the door they had barricaded starting to splinter from the assault of the vampires on the other side.

"We need to hurry," Samantha said. "They're pissed."

Chris opened the last door and stepped into…

Nothing.

The room was empty of any sign of life—or afterlife. There was a desk in the center of the room, messy with papers. A window on the wall looked into the interrogation room. There was a coat rack behind the door. Leather chairs positioned by the desk. Plaques on the wall.

It was as if the office were a perfectly normal setting. Whether to not raise alarm bells of any humans who hadn't been given the vampire bite yet, or simply to imitate humanity, it couldn't be sure. But the "normal" atmosphere was unsettling nonetheless.

"There's nothing here." Holly examined the plaques.

"A dead end." Chris's shoulders sagged. He turned on his wife. "I thought you said they were here? I thought you said that you could sense them?"

She shrugged. "So did I! I don't know where I got that feeling from—but I *still* have it!"

"Then they have to be here somewhere," Samantha said. "Keep searching."

Kathy examined the bookshelf beside the desk. There was something about it that didn't look right. As she inspected it closer, she saw that some of the books were simply props, built into the shelf to make it look as if they were real books.

She pulled on them, expecting one of them to give and the bookshelf to swing open like a door. But none of them budged.

"I think there's something here," she announced to the group. "But I can't figure it out."

"What is it?" Samantha asked.

"I think there might be a door or something behind this shelf."

Chris stepped forward and reached for the shelf. His fingers found the back of it and, with a grunt, he pulled the bookshelf down. It toppled to the floor, crashing into the desk, and spilling the contents of the shelves all over the floor.

The women winced at the noise, but when they looked up, there was a door behind the shelf.

"I knew it!" Kathy said. "No matter what time period you're in, a door behind a bookshelf is always a classic!"

"That must be the gun room that that lady was talking about," Samantha murmured. She went to the door to the office and locked it before returning to the opening behind the bookshelf to inspect further.

Holly stepped on the remaining shelf at the bottom and tried to get the door open. It wouldn't move. "I can't tell if it's locked or sealed."

"What are your powers telling you?" Chris asked his wife.

She closed her eyes and concentrated, placing her palms flat on the board sealing off the doorway. A moment later she opened them. "They're in there. Our kids are in there."

"Then stand back." Chris reached his hand out and helped Holly back down. Then, with a swift gesture of both hands, the board splintered, sending tiny pieces of wood flying everywhere, leaving nothing left where the door had once stood.

"Hopefully that didn't hurt the kids," Holly murmured as she pushed past her husband, holding on to his shoulder to help her up. She was the first to step through into the gun room.

As the rest of them piled in, they saw the kids huddled in the corner. Sophia was holding her younger brother in a tight embrace. But at the sight of her parents, she released that protective hold and allowed her brother to run to his dad.

"Mom! Dad!" Sophia called to them.

"My baby!" Holly cried as she tried to get to her daughter.

As mother stumbled in the tight space to get to her daughter, a hand came out of the corner and snatched Sophia away.

Wilhelm.

"You're too late," he said. "You've already made your decision of which child to save."

CHAPTER 26

The vampires howled as they were incinerated with Chris's magical flames. He stepped out through the doorway, pushing back the remaining vampires into the cubicle office space, pushing them back enough for the women to escape out of the room behind him.

Kathy searched the space for stragglers. Anyone who might be going to get reinforcements. There were two, and she froze them before they could flee through the door.

Then, turning, she saw the remaining vampires lunging at Chris, trying to bite him, but backing off when he wielded flames with his fists. She put up her hands and froze them before they could hurt her nephew.

Samantha and Holly ran to the door the woman in the office

had indicated. Outside, there was a placard that said, Detective Dante Wilhelm.

The door opened easily and they stepped inside, which was a stark contrast from the explosions and commotion out in the outer office area.

Like the room where they had questioned the woman, this office space had a secretary area with several doors off of it.

"Which room is it?" Samantha asked.

"Only one way to find out." Holly went to the first door and opened it. A conference room.

Kathy braced herself against the main door and was soon joined by Chris. After a minute, he moved to push the closest desk in front of the door to better serve as a barricade, since they didn't have a key to the door.

"We'll need to find another way out once we find the kids," Chris said when he was sure the door was secure.

"If the kids are even in here." Holly opened another door to yet another empty office.

The room on the other side of Samantha's door led to the viewing room into the interrogation room, which had another exit that, for now, seemed quiet on the other side. "I may have found a possible way to escape."

"Or a way for more vamps to get in." Kathy came up beside her sister and peered inside. She remembered the harsh interrogation she faced earlier.

"My question is, why is it so empty?" Samantha asked.

"Maybe they've fled to safety," Chris said as he inspected the space, opening desk drawers and examining documents left out. "Or maybe they're trying to lure us into a trap."

Holly nodded. "I sense that the kids are nearby."

Samantha nodded. "Me too. We're getting close."

"But where are they?" Kathy asked.

"We'll find them," Chris said. "Even if I have to tear this whole place apart with my bare hands."

Holly furrowed her brow and looked to Samantha. "Are you picking up on that feeling too?"

Samantha closed her eyes and focused. Her sensing abilities weren't the strength of her specialty, but more a byproduct of it. But she focused and, finally, she locked on to that feeling that Holly had been picking up on too. "Danger."

"Well yeah." Kathy gestured to the door, where the vampires were beating on it from the other side. "That much is obvious."

Holly shook her head. "No, not that. There's another danger. Something we haven't discovered yet."

"The kids?" Samantha asked.

"I think so," Holly said. "They're protected."

"As we suspected," Chris said. "But where?"

Suddenly, as if they were all in sync, their attention collectively focused on the one remaining door that they hadn't passed through yet.

"Could it be that easy?" Kathy asked.

"Only one way to find out." Chris started to the door, but

paused when he heard the door they had barricaded starting to splinter from the assault of the vampires on the other side.

"We need to hurry," Samantha said. "They're pissed."

Chris opened the last door and stepped into…

Nothing.

The room was empty of any sign of life—or afterlife. There was a desk in the center of the room, messy with papers. A window on the wall looked into the interrogation room. There was a coat rack behind the door. Leather chairs positioned by the desk. Plaques on the wall.

It was as if the office were a perfectly normal setting. Whether to not raise alarm bells of any humans who hadn't been given the vampire bite yet, or simply to imitate humanity, it couldn't be sure. But the "normal" atmosphere was unsettling nonetheless.

"There's nothing here." Holly examined the plaques.

"A dead end." Chris's shoulders sagged. He turned on his wife. "I thought you said they were here? I thought you said that you could sense them?"

She shrugged. "So did I! I don't know where I got that feeling from—but I *still* have it!"

"Then they have to be here somewhere," Samantha said. "Keep searching."

Kathy examined the bookshelf beside the desk. There was something about it that didn't look right. As she inspected it closer, she saw that some of the books were simply props, built into the shelf to make it look as if they were real books.

She pulled on them, expecting one of them to give and the bookshelf to swing open like a door. But none of them budged.

"I think there's something here," she announced to the group. "But I can't figure it out."

"What is it?" Samantha asked.

"I think there might be a door or something behind this shelf."

Chris stepped forward and reached for the shelf. His fingers found the back of it and, with a grunt, he pulled the bookshelf down. It toppled to the floor, crashing into the desk, and spilling the contents of the shelves all over the floor.

The women winced at the noise, but when they looked up, there was a door behind the shelf.

"I knew it!" Kathy said. "No matter what time period you're in, a door behind a bookshelf is always a classic!"

"That must be the gun room that that lady was talking about," Samantha murmured. She went to the door to the office and locked it before returning to the opening behind the bookshelf to inspect further.

Holly stepped on the remaining shelf at the bottom and tried to get the door open. It wouldn't move. "I can't tell if it's locked or sealed."

"What are your powers telling you?" Chris asked his wife.

She closed her eyes and concentrated, placing her palms flat on the board sealing off the doorway. A moment later she opened them. "They're in there. Our kids are in there."

"Then stand back." Chris reached his hand out and helped Holly back down. Then, with a swift gesture of both hands, the board splintered, sending tiny pieces of wood flying everywhere, leaving nothing left where the door had once stood.

"Hopefully that didn't hurt the kids," Holly murmured as she pushed past her husband, holding on to his shoulder to help her up. She was the first to step through into the gun room.

As the rest of them piled in, they saw the kids huddled in the corner. Sophia was holding her younger brother in a tight embrace. But at the sight of her parents, she released that protective hold and allowed her brother to run to his dad.

"Mom! Dad!" Sophia called to them.

"My baby!" Holly cried as she tried to get to her daughter.

As mother stumbled in the tight space to get to her daughter, a hand came out of the corner and snatched Sophia away.

Wilhelm.

"You're too late," he said. "You've already made your decision of which child to save."

CHAPTER 27

Out in the inner office, they could hear the vampires clawing at the door to get in. It wasn't barricaded like the door in the outer office had been, so they didn't have as much time to linger. Still, it was a good thing Samantha had locked it when they had first discovered the gun room.

"What do we do?" Kathy asked.

Chris walked to the window behind Wilhelm's desk. He had to step around the books and other tchotchkes that had fallen when he had pulled down the bookshelf hiding the door. He peered out the window. "Looks like it's only about an eight foot drop down to the roof below."

"And then what?" Samantha asked.

He shrugged. "Then we hope there's another escape from there."

"That doesn't sound like a very confident plan," Samantha argued.

The sounds of the scraping and hissing on the other side of the door filled the silence that followed her words.

"It's the best option we have if we're going to survive," Holly said solemnly. She was still, clearly, lost in her own head. Trying to sort through the emotions and the varying levels of grief and loss.

Chris stepped to his wife and tried to pass off Griffin, but the boy clung to his dad.

"No! I want to stay with you!" he whined.

"Just for a minute," Chris insisted. "I have to get the window open." But the boy clung to his father.

Kathy climbed up on what was left of the shelf behind the desk and pulled at the window. It was stuck, so Samantha jumped up to assist. Together, the sisters pulled the window up and then pushed out the screen on the other side.

Kathy stuck her head out the window and looked around. When she came back in, she said, "It looks like a far jump."

"We'll be fine," Samantha assured her—and everyone else. "We really don't have any other choice. Who's going first?"

Chris, who still held Griffin close to him, stepped up.

"No! No! No!" Griffin cried as his father began to climb out the window.

"Are you sure you can manage both of you?" Holly asked.

With the way that Griffin's arms were locked around his

father's neck, Chris could let go long enough to use both hands to hang from the side. After another second, he dropped down below, then called up. "It looks farther than it is!"

Holly was the next to go, jumping out the window without hesitation. Then the sisters stared at each other.

"You go," Samantha said.

Kathy shook her head. "No. You go first. That way, I can freeze the vamps if they break through."

From the sounds of the scratches on the door and the way it seemed to push against the hinges, the vampires were getting close to breaking through.

Samantha nodded at her sister, then climbed out the window.

Kathy watched her go, then heard the crash of the door breaking in. She screamed and put her hands up to freeze the undead before launching herself out the window. She landed with a roll on the roof below. When she righted herself, she felt a twinge of pain in her ankle from the way she had landed. Hopefully just a sprain, but it would slow her down regardless.

"We need to move," she told the group. "They just broke through the door. I froze them but it won't last forever."

Chris was already halfway across the roof. He pointed to an iron ladder that ran down the side of the building. With one hand around his son and the other gripping the ladder, he began to descend.

"Be careful," Holly warned.

"Always," Chris told her.

Each of the witches followed without issue. Down on the ground, they heard the blare of the alarms even louder. The sun was just starting to break through the nighttime darkness with the early morning hour. Still, they could use the remaining shadows to their advantage.

There was grass that separated the short distance between the building and the outer prison wall. Chris stepped to the edge of the building and peered around, then immediately snapped back under the cover of the building.

"Guards," he whispered to the rest of them. "Right over there."

"Now what do we do?" Samantha asked.

They were quiet as they looked around for other options. Then Holly looked over at the prison wall.

"You're going to have to blast through," she said.

"But that'll alert them to our escape," Kathy countered.

"Listen to the alarms," Holly said. "They already know! We'll have to be quick, but it's our only choice."

Chris turned to Kathy. "Get ready to freeze."

Together, the two witches stepped out into the open. Immediately, the guards around the corner noticed them.

"Hey! It's the prisoners! Call Wilhelm!" The one guard charged toward them while the second pulled a radio from his belt to call for backup before following his partner in pursuit of the witches.

THE FATES

Kathy watched nervously as they approached. But a deafening explosion drew her attention to the wall.

At the bottom of the wall was a massive, cracked opening. It looked small, but it would do the trick.

What was more worrying, however, was the giant crack that ran up the length of the wall, all the way to the top. They didn't have much time before the whole thing collapsed.

"We have to move!" Chris called to his family.

Kathy froze the oncoming guard, but saw others pouring out of the building and running toward them.

One-by-one the witches made it through the hole. When it was Kathy's turn to pass through, she heard the shifting rocks from above. More cracks formed in the crumbling wall.

On the other side, Chris motioned them all back away from the wall.

As guards started coming through the hole, Chris waved his hands and blasted the wall again. Heavy rocks and bricks fell before the whole side of the wall came crashing down, crushing the guards under the rubble.

"Up top!" Holly called. She cradled her son close to her and ran into the street, which lined the prison.

At the top of the prison wall were guards with rifles trained on them. They fired, and Kathy put her hands up and froze the bullets. She backpedaled, trying to hurry as fast as she could backwards to escape danger. Her ankle ached with pain, but she tried her best to ignore it. To not let it stop her from escaping.

She felt Samantha's hand on her arm, then looked over and saw her sister concentrating, her eyes trained on the guards.

"What's she doing?" Chris called. "We have to go!"

Kathy put up her hand to shush him.

After several tense seconds, the guards at the top of the wall lowered their weapons and returned to their patrols, as if the prison break hadn't even happened.

Samantha sagged after the exertion of her magic. "I need a good night's sleep."

"Don't we all," Kathy murmured, then ushered Samantha forward to catch up with Chris and Holly, who were already halfway down the street.

With the rising sun, there were no vampires lurking in the shadows, like there had been during their first escape.

Several blocks over, Holly darted down a driveway of an empty house and took cover behind the garage in the backyard of the house. She leaned against the wall and tried to catch her breath, while also soothing Griffin against her chest. Slowly, she sank to the ground.

The others joined her, collapsing onto the weed-filled lawn beside her.

Holly leaned her head against Chris's shoulder as the tears spilled out of her eyes. They both hugged Griffin close as the three of them wept.

"She's gone, Chris," Holly sobbed. "She's gone. Our baby is gone."

He pulled her closer. "I know."

"I can't believe we're going through this again."

Kathy's head picked up at that. She wanted to ask them if they had lost a child before—how much pain did one vampire bite cause? But she didn't want to interrupt the somber moment in their fractured family.

With red eyes, Holly turned to Samantha and Kathy. "You two can fix this."

Kathy felt her eyes—and her expectations—pierce through her. She wanted to reassure the grieving mother, but at this point, she had no idea of what was going to happen next. If they were ever going to get back to their time.

"Promise me that I'll never have to feel this pain again—in *any* timeline," Holly said intensely. "Fix this."

Again, Kathy sat frozen. But Samantha, sympathizing as a mother, nodded. "I will do everything in my power to try to reverse this—and make sure nothing like this can ever happen again."

Then, in a flash of light, Samantha and Kathy were gone.

CHAPTER 28

They reappeared in a completely different world. Their sweaty clothes from running in the hot summer night was suddenly ice cold as the January chill hit them. Their feet crunched over the snow-covered road, and the only lights were the glimmer of the streetlights.

"What happened?" Samantha asked as she hugged herself to keep warm.

"I don't..." Kathy started as she spun around. Then the vision hit her. She was still adjusting to her new power and it struck her like a strong wind. She saw Aldric biting Stockley moments before her and her sister came to stop it. The same vision she had had before. The one that had led to them seeking out the vampire in the first place.

THE FATES

When she came out of the vision, she hunched forward, resting her hands on her knees. The cold didn't bother her at the moment. She was more focused on maintaining her balance.

"What is it?" Samantha asked. "Did you have another vision?"

Since Kathy had received her new power, Samantha had been watchful of her, afraid that her body would reject it like it had more than six months before when a psychic implanted her gift into Kathy.

After regaining her balance, Kathy nodded. "Yeah. This is where we were a couple days ago. Before the Fates came to send us into the future. Where Aldric bit Stockley, and that horrible future began."

Samantha looked around as well. Slowly, she began to nod. "It does look familiar. But I figured the Fates would've talked to us before they reset things."

Kathy scanned the houses on the street and found the one they were supposed to be at. "We thought the Fates weren't even watching anymore." She nodded toward the house. "Come on, we need to move quick."

They ran down the street, feet crunching in the snow. Each of them needed to suppress the exhaustion they felt after their trip to the future. They weren't out of the woods yet.

As they came to the driveway, they saw Aldric leaning in to Stockley. At first glance, it looked as if they were about to kiss, but the witches knew better.

Wasting no time, Kathy grabbed a snow shovel that was propped up against the side of the house and swung it at the back of Aldric's head.

With a loud *crunch* it made contact and the vampire hissed and spun around on Kathy.

Swinging again, Kathy tried to get him in the head once more, but he lifted his arm and evaded the attack. She recovered quickly and struck again, this time making contact with his face and knocking him to the snowy driveway.

"Run!" she called to Stockley.

The nonmagical human looked confused. "But it's my house."

The vampire stirred on the ground. Samantha grabbed Stockley's arm and pulled him away from Aldric's reach.

"Do you have a wooden stake?" she asked.

He raised his eyebrows. "A stake? For what?"

"Don't ask questions! Do you have one?"

As Aldric rose to his feet, Kathy stepped between him and Samantha and Stockley.

"Uh…uh…" Stockley was distracted by the vampire.

Samantha grabbed him by the arms. "Answer me! Do you have one?"

Aldric barred his fangs and hissed at Kathy. She took another swing at him to ward him off.

"A wooden stake? What is this, some kind of vampire hunt or something?"

"Or something. Now go get us something to kill this bastard with!" She watched as Stockley ran inside, afraid that he might call 9-1-1. She debated whether she should follow him, but knew that Kathy would need her help outside.

"Freeze him," Samantha told her sister.

The vampire's speed was incredible. Before Kathy could even lift her hands up to activate her magic, he was right in front of her.

Their eyes met and, despite her best efforts not to, Kathy couldn't keep the terror from her face. This close to the vampire, she saw his red eyes and sickly pale skin. And she could nearly feel his fangs sinking into her flesh.

He grabbed her, but the snow shovel in Kathy's hands got between them, so he shoved her to the ground.

Samantha jumped into action as Aldric jumped on top of her sister. She tried to pull at his arms to prevent him from putting his hands on her but he was freakishly strong—*supernaturally* strong.

More hisses erupted from the vampire as the sisters struggled with him. At one point, he tossed his elbow backward and threw Samantha into a snow bank.

Kathy screamed and kicked beneath Aldric, grateful that the snow shovel provided a sort of barrier between them. Still, in order to keep it in place, it limited her ability to fight back to get him off of her.

Samantha regained her stance and then changed her tactic

to offense. She began to throw punches at the vampire, hitting him in the back, the head, and as many other sensitive areas as she could target from behind. She even tried delivering a kick or two. Nothing seemed to deter the vampire.

With the cold, though, each punch made her hands ache even more. The sisters were not dressed for this weather, making this encounter even more dangerous than just the threat of the vampire.

"Here!"

Samantha hadn't heard Stockley come up beside her, but when she saw what was in his hands, she was glad for his arrival. He held a spade shovel with a wooden handle.

Snatching it from his hands, Samantha began to slam the shovel on the concrete driveway. After several swings, the metal spade broke off, leaving just the wooden handle.

"Hey!" Stockley complained. "I just bought that last summer!"

"Relax!" she barked. "I'll buy you another one!" Turning back to the vampire, she raised the wooden handle and drove it straight into Aldric's back.

Blood poured from Aldric as the stake was driven through his body, right through his heart. Kathy screamed as the blood covered her and she used the snow shovel to push away from him enough to scurry out from beneath him.

Aldric collapsed, fully dead, on the ground. Within seconds, all sign of life left his body and he began to disintegrate into dust that mingled with the snow and blew gently in the cold night breeze.

"*Now* we're in the clear," Samantha told Kathy.

"Hopefully it made the difference that we're hoping for," Kathy added.

"Will someone please tell me what the hell just happened!" Stockley shouted.

Samantha turned to him and said, "That was us keeping you safe."

"And," Kathy added, "saving the future."

CHAPTER 29

Twelve hours of sleep hadn't been enough to make up for the ordeal that Samantha had gone through in the future. Not only had it been physically demanding, but carrying the weight of the world on your shoulders—even for only one day—was a lot to carry. Not to mention the emotional connection she felt for the baby growing in her belly—the one she had connected to so quickly in the future.

The best thing Samantha could do to feel close to her family was lay on the couch and watch cartoons with Josh. Steven had been sitting with them as well, but he grew bored and went upstairs to take a shower.

Samantha, however, couldn't get enough. Usually she had strict rules for how much TV time Josh got, but on this Saturday morning, all rules were thrown out. She needed this moment more than anything.

Her mind kept wandering to the terrible future she and Kathy had seen. The lives that had been lost. The lives that had been *controlled*. The way a dictatorial regime moved in and took over so naturally. Sure, that was aided by vampiric conversion, but it also spoke to how easily manipulated the human race could be sometimes.

She squeezed Josh closer and sunk into the couch. The memories of the future she and Kathy saw scared her for the future world that Josh—and Chris—would one day live in. Hopefully they would be a force of good to maintain a healthy balance.

A commercial for carpet cleaner came on and Josh clumsily slunk down to the floor.

"Where are you going?" Samantha asked him.

He mumbled something that she couldn't make out and then parked himself on the floor beside the couch and played with the entrails of the blanket that covered Samantha.

And then, as she watched him, she saw him stop moving immediately. Then she noticed that the TV had gone silent too. And the roar of the water from Steven's shower upstairs was quiet as well.

"Sammy!" Kathy called as her feet raced down the stairs. "Don't tell me it's happening again!" She hopped down the last two steps and darted into the living room.

By then, Samantha was sitting up and reaching for Josh.

"I wouldn't do that, if I were you." The voice was familiar, but not immediately visible.

As Samantha got to her feet, they appeared. The Fates. Sitting around on the living room furniture, feverishly working away at their knitting, as if they had been sitting there all along.

"Touching him would wake him," one of them said—Clo, from what Samantha remembered.

"And that would alter the timeline," Atro went on.

"And *then* we'd have a mess on our hands," Lakie finished.

"Your son is safe," Clo clarified. "I promise you, that."

"And just so gosh darn *adorable!*" Atro cooed.

"He's going to grow up to be such a good-looking gentleman, I assure you of that," Lakie said.

"Oh, but not a heartbreaker," Atro said. "That's not in his nature."

"We have big plans for him," Clo said.

"Well, that all depends on his free will," Lakie said.

Atro focused on her needles again. "Of course! But we know that he'll make the right choices to lead him in the right direction."

"Oh, Atro, we don't ever really *know* anything!" Clo said with a giggle. "We just hope that he will—"

"What do you three want?" Samantha stood with her hands on her hips and glared at them.

"Yeah, why are you here?" Kathy asked. "We saved the future, didn't we?"

"Haven't you done enough?" Samantha added. "You've already tormented us with a terrible future, when you could've just as easily told us the future was bad and then sent us back in time to fix it. Instead, you had to make it as painful as possible, didn't you? Is that how you get your kicks? Off the misery of others?"

"Sam…" Kathy said quietly.

To Samantha's frustration, Clo smiled. "We tried to tell you just how bad it was."

"You wouldn't believe us," Lakie said.

"So we took extreme measures," Atro added.

"It took a lot of work to create that futuristic scenario." Clo still had her smile.

"We needed to create an environment for you girls to explore in," Lakie explained.

"All to show you why your mistake needed to be corrected," Atro finished.

Kathy narrowed her eyes. "So…if that future was all your creation, does that mean that none of that will come true? Samantha's son and grandkids, passing the house over to them, and…" She trailed off, but Samantha knew what she left unsaid.

Her early death.

"And the hurt, the loss, that our family experiences in the future—that won't happen?" Kathy added.

Finally, Clo turned serious. "Well, some things are predetermined."

Atro nodded. "And as far as the doom and gloom of the version of the future that *you* saw, well, you girls have already reversed that. When you stopped Aldric from biting Stockley."

"And killed Aldric altogether," Lakie added.

Samantha felt the hope growing inside her, but her rational thought told her to be a skeptic. "What do you mean that some things are 'predetermined'? I thought you said that free will trumps any kind of destined path? Are you saying that certain things are meant to happen, regardless of free will? Like people's deaths? Like…" She swallowed the lump forming in her throat. "Like my own early death?"

For once, the Fates weren't quick with the response. The uncomfortable silence hung in the air for several long moments before Atro spoke up.

"Perhaps 'predetermined' was the wrong word. *Likely* is probably the better term."

"But," Lakie jumped in, "just because something is *likely* doesn't mean that free will and the influence of others' free will can't change that likelihood."

Kathy crossed her arms. "So what are you saying?"

"The future is endless with possibilities," Clo said.

"And, thanks to you girls, the world has a much brighter future." Lakie smiled, which was probably meant to cheer up the sisters, but neither of them felt much better.

"So how do you know which outcomes are likely?" Samantha asked. "I mean, *will* I have a son named Chris? Will he marry a woman named Holly?" She indicated her son on the floor. "Will Josh die young? Will *I* die young? Is Steven going to leave me and abandon his children?"

With each question, her voice rose louder and louder until she was nearly shouting. Kathy put an arm around her to settle her and she leaned into it.

Another tense quiet fell over them. The Fates stared at the sisters, their knitting needles resting in their laps and strings of yarn leading down to a shared basket in between them.

"We know you have questions," Atro started.

"But we can't answer any of them for certain," Lakie went on.

"After all, the future hasn't even been created yet." Clo lifted the shared tapestry that they were all working on.

"We're still piecing it together as we go," Atro said.

"Only time will tell what the tapestry weaves," Lakie added.

"We can tell you this," Clo said. "The decisions you make every day will put you in different probabilities for likely outcomes."

"Meaning?" Kathy pressed.

"Meaning that each day, your future changes based on each decision you make," Atro explained.

"So make wise decisions that lead you to a place in life where you want to be," Clo said.

"But how do we know we're making the *right* decisions?" Samantha asked. "I don't want to die young and miss out on my kids' lives!"

"Have faith," Lakie said.

"Follow your heart," Clo added.

"And trust your gut." Atro grinned at her. "It hasn't let you down before."

Samantha and Kathy were both quiet as they took in their advice. The Fates hadn't told them much. Not the concrete answers they had hoped for. Then again, they knew that that hadn't been likely. Still, it would've been nice to know exactly how things were going to play out.

"Well," Clo said after a moment. "We should get going." She turned to the two other Fates. "Are we ready, ladies?"

Each of them returned to their knitting needles. They began to fade away, but then stopped suddenly when Atro put her needles down and looked at the sisters.

"Oh, by the way," she said. "Don't be surprised if your memory of the future fades as time goes on."

"You mean we're going to *forget* it all?" Kathy blurted. "After all that!"

"I know," Lakie said sympathetically. "It's only natural for you to want to enjoy the good moments in those memories. The times you spent with your future children, chief among them."

"But we can't risk altering your choices through free will based on your knowledge of the future," Clo said.

The Fates

"However," Atro said, "as a thank you for correcting the mistake, your memories will fade *slowly* over time."

"Thanks again!" Lakie added as each of the Fates returned to their knitting and began to fade again.

"Wait!" Samantha hollered after them. "How much will we remember?"

"When will we forget?" Kathy added.

But it was too late. The Fates were gone.

CHAPTER 30

Samantha eyed the wine list and wished that she could indulge for one evening. After the week she had had, she deserved a drink.

But the Fates' words still rang in her head. She needed to make good decisions going forward so that she could put herself in a position to have positive outcomes in the future.

Having a drink during pregnancy was not a road she wanted to go down. Not if it would put her child in any kind of danger at all.

"I think this was the better night to go to dinner anyway." Steven's voice broke into her thoughts.

"Yeah. This is nice. I'm glad we came."

It was their second attempt at their anniversary dinner. Two years married. They were supposed to go out the night before, but Samantha and Kathy had to go try to kill a vampire, fail, then travel to the future and see how bad that mistake was, then go back and kill the vampire again.

She was tired.

But she had made a promise to Steven that they would try again the next day to go to dinner, as much as Samantha wanted to just sit at home and cuddle with Josh and Steven on the couch. But in order to protect Steven, she hadn't told him about her trip to the future. There was no sense in it if Samantha herself was going to forget someday. And part of her new resolve was to focus on the things that mattered: her family. Steven was a part of her family.

"It's crazy that it's been two years," he said. "Feels like we just got engaged."

Samantha thought the opposite. While she knew her marriage was still in the early years, it felt like they had lived so much life in those two years that if someone had told her it had been ten years instead, she would've believed them.

"You remember when we first got engaged and you had no idea that I was a witch?" she asked in a hushed tone.

Steven huffed a laugh. "Yeah…"

"When I did tell you, I thought for sure that we were over." She kicked herself for the comment. What great anniversary talk, reminding themselves of the time that they almost broke up.

He soured a little. "Yeah. Wasn't my finest hour."

She shrugged. "You had to come to terms with it. And you did. But it took time."

"And you almost dying."

She rolled her eyes and smirked. "Happens all the time."

He raised his eyebrows. "Yeah, but I had no idea how much at that time." He smiled and shook his head, then reached for her hand. "In the end I made the right choice."

She returned his smile and let him steer the conversation back to more appropriate anniversary territory.

"And what a wild—and wonderful—two years it has been," he added.

"One kid, another on the way—we move quick, Steven Harper."

"I had to lock you down so you didn't slip away," he said. "And I'm glad I did." He grew more serious, then added, "I know that I complain about your magic a lot—and I wish it didn't complicate our lives as much as it does, but there's no one else I'd rather navigate all of that with than you."

She squeezed his hand back. "I know. I feel the same way. You're the one, Steven. As annoying as you are, you're the one."

They both broke into laughter. No, marriage hadn't been easy. But so far, it had certainly been worth it. Samantha only hoped that it continued to be worth it. The only way to make certain of that was to keep trying. Keep showing up and putting in the work.

"Oh! Ouch! Well, hopefully Josh doesn't pick up on your bad habits, either," he said with a laugh. "Then I'd have two of you to deal with."

"Well, if you think our lives are chaotic now, just wait until we have *two* boys running around the house," Samantha said. "And with them being so close in age, I think the volume level in our house is going to increase significantly."

Steven didn't join in her laughter. Instead, he looked at her with a smile and a hint of surprise. "Boy? We're having another boy?"

She made a face. That was a slip of the tongue. Keeping the secret about her trip to the future was going to be harder than she thought.

"The baby is the size of a pea or something. How do you know? The doctor doesn't even know yet! I don't think the baby's even developed that—" He stopped and squinted at her. "This is somehow magic-related, isn't it?"

Another cringe. "It's a long story."

Steven saw the waiter coming over with their food. "Well then." He fanned out his napkin and lay it on his lap. "It's a good thing we have a whole meal to talk about it. And, if you play your cards right, I'll spring for dessert too."

As the waiter laid out their food for them and asked if they needed anything else, Samantha sat back and admired her husband. She was lucky to have him. *Happy* to have him. In the moment, she was happy.

Even if her future didn't pan out the way she dreamt that it would, she was lucky to have these happy moments. If she was going to keep them, she needed to celebrate them. Each and every one.

After all, fate was really in her hands.

Kathy and her sister, Samantha, have always been a team. Throughout their time as witches, they've taken out more than their share of bad guys. But after Kathy meets Will, who she learns is a demonic Dark Knight, her loyalties begin to change.

Meanwhile, Samantha doesn't trust Will or his intentions. Still, Kathy can't help but feel tempted by the dark side as she falls deeper in love with Will. Crossing over would give Kathy the freedom to do whatever she wanted with her magic. No rules. No limitations. It would also mean breaking the bond she has always shared with her sister, who has made it clear that she wants nothing to do with the dark side.

When Will proposes they take over the underworld, Kathy loves the idea of having power. But it also leaves her with a choice that will change her life: abandon her family and the life she has always known, or give up the love of her life forever.

The Full Moon is the first book in the Under the Moon series, which is a part of the Art of Magic universe, containing the Lost By Magic and the Coven series.

THE FULL MOON

UNDER THE MOON: BOOK 1

Read on for an excerpt of the first book in
the Under the Moon series, a sequel series
to the Coven series!

DAVID NETH

CHAPTER 1

- APRIL 2005 -

Hold the elevator!" Kathy raced through the lobby with her bag slung over her shoulder. She was trying not to trip in her heels.

The men and women in the crowded elevator ignored her, pretending to not see her racing through the lobby like a madwoman. Luckily, a man held out his hand in between the doors just as they were about to close. He was wearing a black suit that fit him perfectly. Kathy was surprised. It was a rare sight to see a man dressed so nicely. But then, she had never really gone to an office building like this before. Her prior experiences with men were the try-too-hard Abercrombie type. And she was definitely over those guys.

She was glad that she had at least one good suit of her own.

The Full Moon

It wasn't exactly a suit, but the gray between the jacket and the skirt matched so perfectly that nobody noticed. She checked out the other women in the elevator with her and judged how much they spent on their outfits. More money than she had, certainly.

"Thank you!" Kathy smiled and repositioned the bag on her shoulder. She hit the button for the fifth floor and squeezed in next to the man.

"Of course. I never mind sharing an elevator with a pretty lady like yourself." He smiled.

Kathy rolled her eyes and noticed how many other people did the same. He was certainly trying to charm her, but she would've been lying if she said it didn't help. Especially when she was already stressing out. She smiled at him briefly and then fixed her eyes on the display above the elevator doors that read which floor they were on. With the amount of people on the elevator, it was no surprise that it stopped at every floor. She grumbled at the people who got off on the second floor. Couldn't they take the stairs? The doors opened on the fourth floor and the man stepped out.

"I hope you have a wonderful day," he said as he exited the elevator.

Kathy smiled and muttered, "You too."

Soon she stepped out onto the fifth floor and searched for Johnson & Cramer, Inc.

The hallway was bland, nothing like the beautiful lobby on the first floor, with cream walls and no signs directing where each business was located. She stepped away from the elevator and decided to take a left, searching for the correct office. She reached the end of the hall and still hadn't found it so she turned, passed the elevator again, and went in the opposite direction, finally finding the place.

There wasn't anyone at the front desk, so she tapped the little bell on the counter and waited. Soon a man in a loose-fitting gray suit walked out of his office with a to-go cup of coffee from the café downstairs. His blazer gaped open and unbuttoned and his belly hung over his belt.

"You here for the interview?"

Kathy extended her hand with a smile—one she'd practiced with her sister the night before—and said, "Yes. I'm Kathy Walker. So nice to meet you. Are you Mr. Johnson or Mr. Cramer?"

The man chuckled. "No, they're both dead." Her face flushed with embarrassment, but she smiled and tried to play it off. The man shook Kathy's hand and then took a sip of his coffee. "I'm Richard Burke. I'm the sales manager. Why don't you come in my office and we can chat?"

Kathy nodded and followed him.

"Have a seat," he offered with an extended hand as he looped around to his seat behind his desk. Papers littered it, except for the area on the corner of the desk to his left where his computer sat. "I had a chance to take a look at your résumé." He sighed. "Honestly, I was a little underwhelmed. You have very little job experience. My concern is that if I hired you to be my assistant, you wouldn't be able to keep up with the work."

Kathy's stomach lurched. This guy cut right to the chase. "Yeah, I…um…well, I have been out of work for a bit, helping my sister raise her kids. She has two boys." Since Samantha's husband left her last month, she had been her sister's support at home. But now that Steven's paycheck wasn't coming in, Kathy needed to chip in financially, too.

Richard looked down at his copy of her résumé.

Her last job had been at the gas station. She worked the overnights and saw her fair share of weirdos. "Well, officially," she added as he scanned her résumé. "In that time I've been working under-the-table a bit."

Richard leaned back in his chair and rocked back and forth, his right leg crossed over his left. He balanced his coffee on his bent knee and held the foot resting on his knee with his free hand. "Yeah? What kind of work was that?"

Kathy hesitated. "I was working at a hotel downtown, occasionally."

"Front desk?" There was optimism in his voice.

"Um…actually, more in the entertainment…business." She saw his eyebrows scrunch together in confusion and pressed on. "They hired me as a psychic. Actually, in that position I was able to learn some great communication and customer service skills that I think would be useful to me at a job like this." She was hoping she could spin her desperate stint at the hotel into something positive.

Richard smiled. "Miss Walker, I appreciate your enthusiasm for this position, but I'm afraid you aren't qualified enough. I have interviews lined up with other applicants with years of experience working in a secretarial position who would make excellent assistants. I'm sorry, but I don't think this is going to work out."

Kathy gave him a curt smile and reached for her bag on the side of her chair. "Well, I appreciate you taking the time to meet with me. Good luck filling the position."

"Well, hold on a minute, Miss Walker," Richard said. He stood and walked to the door, closing it. "I believe I could free up some room on the payroll, if you'd be willing to do some…extracurricular work." He stepped closer to her and reached for her hand.

She backed away from him until she was up against the wall.

"You'd have the same salary, benefits, everything. I'm sure I could find something around here for you to do." He placed his hand on her hip and moved closer.

She put her hands on his chest and pushed him back. "Mr. Burke, I may be unqualified for this position, but I'm not stupid. I'm not going to be your office whore so you can feel like a man."

"Whoa, sweetie—"

"*Don't* call me 'sweetie.'" She moved to exit, but he grabbed her arm. "Let go of me, Mr. Burke."

"I'm sure we can sort something out," he pushed.

THE FULL MOON

Kathy whipped her arm around, breaking free of his hold. She held up her other hand, and he stopped moving, frozen in place. With a deep breath, she contemplated kicking him to prove her point but decided against it.

Instead, she opened the door and exited his office. One of the insurance agents by the front desk asked how the interview went.

"Your boss is a pervert," Kathy stated. She repositioned her bag, hooked her thumb on the strap, and walked to the elevator.

On her way down, the elevator stopped once more on the fourth floor and the man in the black suit stepped in.

"You know you can't live in the elevator, right?"

Kathy rolled her eyes and ignored him.

"Bad day?"

She nodded.

"Care to unload it on a complete stranger over lunch?"

She looked up at him. "Right now? Don't you have to work?" She had only been at the interview for fifteen minutes, max. Didn't this guy have anything better to do than ride the elevator all day?

He shrugged. "Yeah. Unless you have other plans."

Kathy wanted to say no, but she was not one to believe in coincidences. This was the second random encounter with this man today. It had to mean something. "Sure, all right."

"Yeah? Do you have a preference on a place to go? You seem like an easy-to-please girl."

Sidestepping his comment, Kathy suggested the café downstairs.

"Sounds good to me." He held out his hand. "I'm Will, by the way."

"Kathy." His grip was firm and his smile was charming, but she was sure this would be the last she saw of him. She had no intention of ever showing her face in this office building again.

They ordered at the counter, and the woman who helped them already had Will's dish ready to go when they arrived.

"I called from upstairs. This is my usual go-to place for lunch," he explained.

"Oh. Did you want to go somewhere else?" Kathy asked.

"No, I like it here."

After Kathy ordered, they took a seat at a table by the window.

"So do you care to spill about your lousy, horrible, no good, rotten day, or do you want me to help you forget about it?" Will asked.

Kathy smiled, stirring her spoon in her soup. "I had a job interview for an assistant position at Johnson & Cramer…basically a glorified secretary."

"I'm guessing it didn't go well?" Will took a bite of his wrap.

"Besides the fact that I have no relevant job experience and that I've essentially been unemployed for the last six years, the guy was a real dick," Kathy blurted. She sat back and took a deep breath. "Sorry."

THE FULL MOON

Will held up his hands in a surrender gesture and said, "I know. Bad day."

"And now I have to go home and tell my sister that I screwed this up," she continued. She absently stirred her spoon in her soup. Being the hotel psychic wasn't really a lucrative job, but it helped. Now that the hotel was under new management, Kathy had been the first to go. Samantha had been nagging her since then to find another job.

"You're supposed to eat it," Will joked, indicating her soup. Kathy cracked a smile and let go of her spoon. "Look on the bright side: you were still able to walk out of there with your head held high. And hey, you still have your *incredibly* good looks."

"Apparently that's all I'm good for." She turned her attention out the window at the crowd walking on the sidewalk. They had jobs and families and places to be. For a moment, Kathy envied them.

Will wiped his hands and looked at her. "That's not what I meant…"

"I know. But that's what Richard Burke was looking for. Some office fun," Kathy said. "I'm sorry. I shouldn't be telling you all this. You work in the same building as him."

"Richard Burke?"

Kathy nodded.

"That man is a snake! His last secretary left after suing him for sexual harassment! If I knew you were going there, I would've warned you!" He tossed his napkin on the table. "I'm going to straighten him out."

"No! I already took care of it." She wondered if her magic still had its hold on him. She didn't want Will walking in on a magically frozen Burke. Even if she planned on never seeing him again.

"You're right." Will relaxed. "You don't need anyone to fight your battles for you. You certainly look like you can take care of yourself. But please, eat."

Kathy smiled and brought a spoonful to her mouth. Her first bite to eat since breakfast. "Wow, this is good!"

He smiled. "Right? That's why it's my daily favorite."

She ate a bit more and asked, "So where do you work?"

"I actually am in charge of a small law firm up on the fourth floor. William Brown Attorneys."

"Wow! That's incredible!"

"Yeah, it's pretty nice being my own boss and all. Right now it's just me and another lawyer friend of mine, so a lot of the housekeeping stuff like finances, phone calls, meetings, they're all done by me. Well, pretty much."

"Are you looking for a secretary?" Kathy smiled.

"Do you know someone?"

"Maybe." Kathy broke up some crackers in what was left of her soup.

"I know who you're talking about. I heard she's completely unqualified." He smiled.

The Full Moon

"Too soon!" Kathy laughed and tossed a bit of her cracker at him.

He put his hands up in another surrender gesture and said, "I'm kidding. But really, I would love to hire you, but the money just isn't there yet. Hopefully soon. I'll definitely keep my eyes open for you, though."

"How are you going to reach me if you find something?" Kathy took a spoonful of the rest of her soup. As thick as he was laying it on, she was surprised he hadn't weaseled her number out of her sooner.

"I was hoping this would be a sly way to get your number."

"You think it's that easy, huh?" Kathy laughed.

"Well, I did buy you lunch," Will prodded, flashing a smile. "And I've been a shoulder to cry on in this devastating time of your life."

Kathy rolled her eyes again. "Oh, what a gentleman. Do you have a pen?"

"Of course." He opened his jacket and pulled a gold ballpoint pen out of the inside pocket. It had the name of his business branded on the side.

"You can't afford a secretary, but you can buy novelty pens?" Kathy scribbled her name and number on a fresh napkin. She couldn't believe she was doing this. The last time she'd given a guy a number like this she had been drunk. She'd needed to change her number in order to get him and his buddies to stop calling.

"It's called *branding*. Some expenses are worth it," Will explained. "Plus, I can write it off."

Kathy smiled and slid the napkin over to him. "Don't give this to your college buddies for a late-night booty call. I have caller ID."

Will folded it and placed it in the pocket inside his jacket. He placed his hand over it and declared, "I will protect this to the death."

Kathy laughed. Her day was turning out to be better than where it was originally heading.

Will glanced at his watch. "Oooh, I have to go. I have a meeting with a client in half an hour and I haven't prepared for it yet. Can I walk you to your car?"

Kathy cringed. Her best self was not coming across. "I don't have a car, actually. You could walk me to the bus station, but it's about three blocks away."

"Where do you live?"

"Just on the edge of the city on Arlington. Not exactly easy walking, especially in these shoes." Kathy stuck out her foot so Will could see the artificial height she was walking on.

"I see that." He stood and offered his hand to help her up. "I will walk you to the bus stop, but I'm afraid I won't be able to wait with you."

Kathy took his hand and stood. For a moment they were nearly pressed up against each other until Will took a step back. "Won't you be late for your meeting?"

The Full Moon

"I'm my own boss, remember? I think it's worth it. I want to make sure your day only gets better from here."

"You're really working it, huh?" Kathy said, leading him out of the café and in the direction of the bus stop.

"Is it working?"

"Maybe you should try that number to find out," Kathy suggested. They crossed the intersection and she reached for her ear. "I think I lost an earring."

Will looked around the sidewalk. "I'll check the other side."

She grabbed his arm to stop him and said, "It's not a big deal. I have more."

When they reached the bus stop, they both hesitated, unsure how to properly say good-bye.

"Thank you for lunch."

"It was my pleasure," Will said. "Good luck on your job search, and I will definitely be keeping my eye open for you."

Will moved to kiss her cheek and ran into Kathy's extended hand. They laughed and settled on a wave.

Kathy watched as Will walked back to the office building. She couldn't help but smile. All things considered, it was a very good day.

CHAPTER 2

Kathy gulped down a glass of water after her morning run. She had taken her nephews to school and had already thrown in a load of laundry. Her goal for the day was to set up a couple more job interviews. Her sister, Samantha, had helped her tweak her résumé to make it look more professional. Kathy hoped the changes would do the trick. She also hoped that she never met another interviewer like Richard Burke, but she knew that was likely a fantasy.

She grabbed a hand towel from the stove and wiped away the sweat beading up on her forehead. She had just kicked off her sneakers when the doorbell rang.

Kathy peered through the stained glass on the front door, trying to make out who it was. It was not unusual to get unexpected or uninvited guests. She relaxed a bit when she saw a suit coat and tie. Anything that was looking to kill her or her family was not usually dressed so nicely.

"Good morning." It was Will. Kathy flashed him a smile and then realized that she looked like a mess. A complete opposite of what she'd looked like the last time she'd seen him. Instead of a gray pinstripe suit coat and skirt, she wore a pink tank top and black shorts. Her hair was matted with sweat, and she was sure she stank, too.

"Hi," Kathy responded, a little confused. "How do you know where I live?"

"You told me Arlington, remember?"

She ran her hand along the top of her head, hoping to smooth out a few escaped hairs from her ponytail. It still didn't make sense. She had only met Will once and here he was on her doorstep.

Finally, Will sighed. "Okay, I cheated. I asked a neighbor. Told her you were a friend of mine from college."

Kathy pointed to the house across the street. "Mrs. Kors?" Kathy's busybody neighbor was always looking for reasons to check in or get the latest gossip. As a retired woman in her 70s, she frequently binged on the latest scoop.

"The short old woman across the street?" He tossed a thumb behind him. "She seemed sweet."

"That's the one." She folded her arms across her chest and asked, "So…what are you doing here?"

"Well I bought you lunch last week, I just figured it was your turn to return the favor." He flashed another charming smile. Kathy cocked an eyebrow. "I'm kidding, unless you're offering." He paused to see if she would bite. When she didn't, he continued, "What I came here for was to return this." He held out his hand. Sitting in the middle of his palm was the earring Kathy had lost the day of her interview.

"Where'd you find it?" She scooped it up and studied it, making sure it was the same one.

"One of the girls at the café found it. They thought it might belong to you since it was at my usual seat," Will explained.

"Well, it was very nice of you to return it. Thank you," Kathy said. She gripped the door and made to close it, but Will's voice stopped her.

"Would you like to go to dinner sometime?"

Kathy stopped and looked at him before answering. Her knee-jerk reaction was to say no. She knew she wasn't exactly a catch. Unemployed and living with her sister, who was a single mother of two. The only thing going for her was her looks, and she knew that whenever a guy spontaneously asked her out, he was rarely looking for a meaningful relationship. However, the more she looked at Will, the more she found herself forgetting all her previous experience with men.

"On a date?"

Will tilted his head sideways and nodded shyly. "I was hoping."

The Full Moon

They considered each other for a moment. A crash from the kitchen broke Kathy's trance. She knew her sister wouldn't be home all day, and it was too early for the boys.

"Um…sure, yeah, I will." She looked back into the house and then back at Will. She needed to get rid of him, fast. The noise was likely an attack, and she didn't want Will caught in the crossfire, nor did she want her secret exposed.

"Is everything all right?" He stepped forward, but Kathy pushed him away.

"Yeah, it's fine. Look, you have my number, so call me and we'll set something up." She closed the door farther and farther as she spoke. "Bye!"

Once the door was shut, she raced to the kitchen. She saw a puddle of water by the sink but no sign of an intruder. Grabbing a knife, she crept through the house. She stopped when she stepped in another puddle of water in the living room, which soaked into her socks. Looking around on the floor for a trail of water to indicate where the trespasser was, she tensed up when she felt a drop of water on her neck. She looked up and gasped.

A slimy fishlike creature perched upside down on the vaulted ceiling. Covered in scales and fins lining the middle of his head and down his back, he bared his razor-sharp teeth and hissed when Kathy spotted him. His long claws dug into the wall, holding him in place.

After a moment of hesitation, he lunged at Kathy. She slipped on the puddle as she tried to escape and fell to the ground. The creature caught her ankle in his slimy grasp and pulled her toward him. Kathy managed to grab on to the front parlor door frame and used her other foot to swing around and kick the beast in the face.

Back on her feet, she snatched up the knife and drove it into the creature's chest. Despite being impaled, the creature let out a roar and swatted at Kathy, scratching her arm and drawing blood.

She scrambled up the stairs and to her bedroom, slamming the door behind her. She searched for something she could use to contain him or slow him down.

Kicking open the door, the creature hissed once again at Kathy before stepping into the room. Out of options, she nabbed her hair dryer, and firing it up to full blast, she pointed it at the creature. He sent out another hiss and jumped out of the hallway window and down to the yard. Kathy watched as he jumped over the fence and down the street. She swore to herself, knowing there was no way she would be able to catch him on her own.

* * *

I'm home!" Samantha announced as she walked through the front door.

"We're in the kitchen!" Kathy called. She was pulling a pan out of the oven. "And dinner's ready!" It was a chicken left over from another meal that Samantha had made a few weeks before. All Kathy needed to do was pull it out of the freezer and stick it in the oven.

"Oooh, perfect timing!" Samantha hooked her keys by the door and kissed each of her boys on the head. They were at the kitchen table doing homework. Sixteen-year-old Josh, Samantha's oldest, was the main reason his brother, Chris, who was fourteen, finished any of his homework at all. "How was your day, boys?"

"Good," they droned.

Once the table was cleared of textbooks and notebooks, Kathy, Samantha, and the boys sat down for dinner.

"Any luck with your job hunt?" Samantha asked her sister. She cut into her chicken and took a bite.

"Y'know, I started the day off great. Very productive, but some things happened and it just didn't turn out," Kathy said. She knew Samantha didn't like to talk about demonic attacks too much in front of the boys. The attacks were inevitable, but Samantha wanted her children to be as normal as possible without being scarred by whatever was hiding in their closets.

Kathy thought the whole idea was stupid. The boys would need to know how to use their magic to protect themselves eventually. It was only a matter of time before they were targeted. But they were Samantha's kids, so Kathy tried to keep talk of demonic activity to a minimum.

As a result, the sisters often used ridiculous excuses to evade any magic talk. Kathy was sure the boys didn't buy it, though. Josh and Chris were young, not stupid. They were smarter than Samantha sometimes gave them credit for.

"I noticed the laundry didn't get done," Samantha pressed.

"But I mopped the floor," Kathy countered.

"And she made dinner," Josh added. The sisters bickered a lot, especially now that Kathy wasn't bringing in any money. Josh remembered how much arguing there was in the house when his dad was still around. So now he always tried to calm the storm before it turned into something bigger.

Hearing her son's tone, Samantha gave in. "Yes, you're right. Thank you, Kathy." She turned to her youngest son and asked, "Did you finish your homework?"

"I just have a couple of math problems left, but they shouldn't take me long," Chris said. He attempted to shove a giant spoonful of mashed potatoes in his mouth.

"Smaller bites, Chris, c'mon," Samantha said. She thought back to the days when their father had been there to help her out. It made her sad to think that Steven could so easily abandon his family. His children.

When dinner was over, Samantha and Kathy started on the dishes as the boys finished their homework.

"There was an attack today," Kathy whispered to her sister. "And I didn't get him."

Samantha put down the plate she was drying and turned to Josh and Chris.

The Full Moon

"Boys, would you mind finishing upstairs in your room? Your aunt and I need to discuss some stuff," Samantha said.

"Are you going to talk about magic? I want to help!" Chris loved magic, despite not having any active powers of his own.

Samantha tried not to lie to the boys, so it was difficult for her to respond truthfully when they asked her outright about magic. "Yes, we are. But right now I need you to finish your homework." She smiled at him. "We'll come to you guys if we need help."

Chris sighed and left the room with Josh. Samantha knew the boys—especially Chris—were anxious to be in the midst of the action, but it would be too soon before they were. She wanted to protect them as long as she could, but she also needed to prepare them for any attack that might happen if she or Kathy wasn't around. Now that they were getting older, it was getting harder and harder to keep them in someone's company for their protection.

Once the boys were gone, Samantha pressed Kathy for more details. Her sister dried her hands and pulled the magic book out from the pantry.

"I was looking through it when the boys came home," Kathy explained. "I really don't think we should hide it from them this much. They should know that at any minute we could be attacked."

"I don't want them to be terrified their whole lives. They're just kids," Samantha said.

"They're teenagers, they're not helpless," Kathy countered. She flipped to a page in the book. "Anyway, this is the guy who attacked me."

"Vepar?"

Kathy nodded and pointed to a warning in the entry. "This scared me."

Samantha read from the book: "'If his blood mixes with anyone else's, they too will become a creature like him.' Did he bleed on you?"

Kathy shook her head. "No, but he scratched me pretty good." She showed off her wounded arm. "His blood didn't mix with mine, but I got some of his slime in there. I thought that might add to the mutation process, but I think I'm good."

"Why didn't you call me?" Samantha gripped her sister's elbow and examined her arm. "What would've happened if the boys came home and you were some fish-mutant?"

"Plus side? I'm not. And the book has a potion that'll help kill him," Kathy said.

"Okay." Samantha let go of Kathy's arm and looked at the entry in the book. "So do you have anything of his that we can track him with?"

Kathy bit her lip. "No. I didn't think of it. I mopped up the mess so the boys wouldn't see, and that was all he had leftover. But he freaked out when I shot my hair dryer at him, so I'm guessing he can't stay out of the water that long."

"Kathy! It's going to be impossible to find him!"

THE FULL MOON

"Why? I just figured he'd be in the lake. We head out to Presque Isle and look for him. Simple as that. He'll probably want to stay away from people, so a beach in April is perfect."

Samantha tucked her dark hair behind both of her ears and crossed her arms. The same stance she took whenever the boys were making poor arguments to get out of housework and she was getting frustrated with them. Kathy didn't appreciate Samantha treating her like one of the kids.

"Think about it, Kathy. Do you know how many people in Erie have a swimming pool? By April they still have them closed, which means they're not using them. Not to mention that it rains a lot this time of year, so he could probably rehydrate himself without entering a large body of water. And what about if he hurts someone before we can find him?"

Kathy held up her hands. "All very good points. But look, I actually saw this thing with my own eyes. He's not that intelligent. Someone sent him. He's not going to hurt anybody unless whoever is in charge of him orders him to do it. Since he came here looking for me, I'm most likely the target."

Samantha sighed and leaned back on the counter. "Okay. But I still think it's a good idea to equip every one of us— including the boys—with this potion so that, just in case you're not the sole target, we are all protected."

Kathy smirked. "You're going to corrupt the minds of your tiny children? How will they survive!?" She laughed and Samantha shot her a look.

"Finish the dishes. I'll start heating water."

They began preparing the potion, dropping in the various ingredients the book called for. They only had to substitute a few, but Samantha was very confident in her potion-making abilities and knew the substitutions wouldn't be a problem.

"So why do you think you're the target?" Samantha asked. She was waiting for the potion to thicken before adding the next ingredient.

Kathy shrugged and continued with the dishes. "I don't know. Maybe it's the whole family? I was just the only one home. I know several people are dying to get their hands on the book. Or it could be our powers. You never know with these things."

"True. Which is why we need to be extra careful. We don't know enough about this guy," Samantha said.

"Yeah, but I don't think we should put our lives on hold just because we get attacked." Kathy set a dish in the drying rack. "We should still go to work, go shopping, go on dates, see friends…you know…"

Samantha raised her eyebrows and smiled. "Do you have something you want to tell me?"

She could always tell when Kathy was seeing someone new. She acted like a teenager every time she was about to go on a first date. Still, it had been a while since Kathy was this lovesick. She began giving up on men once she saw the pain Steven had inflicted on Samantha when he left. Samantha was glad to see that Kathy was getting over her fear of getting hurt like she did.

The Full Moon

Kathy shrugged. "Last week when I was at that crappy job interview, this guy I met in the elevator asked me to lunch—"

"You meet guys in the most random places!"

"I wasn't putting out! It was just lunch!" Kathy was smiling. A week had passed since she'd first met Will Brown, and she barely thought of him. Now she couldn't help smiling whenever she did. "Anyway, he showed up this morning and asked me out."

"House call?"

"I lost an earring." Kathy knew what her sister was implying.

Samantha smiled and added the next ingredient. "All right, this thing is just about done. Let me go warn the boys."

"They'll be fine, Sammy. Don't worry about it too much."

CHAPTER 3

Kathy's phone buzzed on the table for the third time that morning.

"Are you ever going to answer that?" Chris asked. He was lifting the bowl of sugary milk leftover from his cereal to his mouth.

Kathy silenced her phone. "I know what he's calling for, and I don't have an answer yet."

"Is it your lawyer?" Samantha was spreading butter on a bagel.

Kathy rolled her eyes and smiled. "He's not *mine*. But yeah, it's him."

"Have you gone out yet?" Samantha asked.

Kathy shook her head. "Not yet."

The Full Moon

Josh held a piece of toast between his teeth and slid his books into his backpack. When his hand was free, he took a bite and asked, "What are you waiting for?"

"With Vepar attacking at any minute, I don't want to risk bringing someone home and exposing our secret. Or accidentally getting him killed," Kathy explained. Samantha shot her a look so she added, "Not that anyone's dying. We just have to be careful, that's all."

Samantha was eager to change the subject. "Do you boys have your potions?"

Chris waved it in the air. "Got it!" He slipped it into his pocket.

"Don't get it taken away this time, okay? I used the last of the mugwort in that batch." The last time the boys had needed to take a potion to school, Chris kept playing with it in class and it had been confiscated by the teacher. That had been a tough one to explain.

"All right, get your things." She shot a glance at the clock. "Oooh, I didn't realize it was so late already. We need to go." She popped the last bite of her bagel in her mouth, wiped her hands on her napkin, and rushed out the door with Josh and Chris in tow.

When her sister and her nephews shuffled out of the house, Kathy stood from her seat to tackle the dishes. Just as she filled the sink, her phone rang again.

It was Will. Again. She stared at it for a moment, deciding

whether or not she should answer it. She wanted to go out with him, but she didn't know how to tell him that she was putting off their date on account of his safety. She didn't want to give him the impression that she was blowing him off. After going back and forth in her mind, she finally dried her hands and answered at the last second.

"I'm so sorry I haven't gotten back to you," Kathy started before he could say anything.

"Are you even still interested? I asked you out a week ago, and I haven't spoken to you since. I thought I might've had the wrong number." His deep, warm voice was a very nice sound to hear that early in the morning. Kathy couldn't help but smile and wonder what was wrong with her.

She cringed and tried to keep a casual tone. "Yeah, sorry. It's been a crazy week. But my nights are basically free the rest of this week." As long as Samantha was home to watch the boys, she wouldn't have to worry too much about an attack from Vepar. Her sister would definitely call if something happened. They each had the potion, so all that they needed to do was wait it out. There hadn't been any strange reports, so obviously Vepar wasn't on a killing spree.

"How's tonight?"

"Tonight?" Her voice betrayed her with a squeak. She cleared it and said, "Um…yeah, that could work."

"I hope you're in the mood for seafood. There's this great restaurant at the hotel on the bay," Will said.

THE FULL MOON

Kathy's mind snapped to her intermittent stints as the hotel psychic. She knew that hotel—and that restaurant—*very* well. Showing her face there would be embarrassing, but she didn't want to tell him no again. "Perfect."

"Great! I'll pick you up at six?"

"You already know where I live, so sounds good."

* * *

As Will and Kathy walked into the hotel, he apologized for having to park so far away. There was an event at the convention center on the next pier over, taking up all the area parking. They'd managed to find street parking but still ended up walking six blocks.

"Will, it's fine. It's not your fault." She wore a sleeveless red satin dress with black heels. By the time they reached the hotel, her feet were happy to be resting. They were certainly not hiking shoes.

Will ordered for the two of them. Kathy didn't hear what it was he ordered—for dinner or for wine. When he saw her concerned face, he said, "You'll like it. Trust me."

She smiled and took a sip of her water. "So, how's the practice?"

"Good, actually. I signed another client just today. Her case doesn't seem to be too hard, but I guess we'll see what the defense has when we get to court," he said. "How's the job hunt?"

"Horrible." She took another sip of her water nervously. The fancy hotel with seafood and wine, it was not her typical style. These weren't her type of people. She felt like a fake for trying to be like them. She usually set up in the front lobby, dressed in her most festive psychic attire and asking folks if they'd like to know their future. She set her glass on the table and took a deep breath. "Have you heard of any openings for me?"

"You see, I realized later that I don't know much about you," he said with a smile. "I'd like to change that."

Kathy looked him in the eyes. She liked him. He had potential, that much she knew, but she wanted to be sure he understood just what he was getting into. From what she could tell, Will was used to elegant seafood dinners. The piano playing softly in the corner didn't strike him as too much. Kathy was used to heating up ramen in the microwave and watching TV while slurping up her noodles on the couch. She needed to set the record straight before either of them got in too deep. "Actually, my last job was at this hotel."

"Oh, really? Front desk?"

She smiled briefly and said, "Hotel psychic. I wasn't exactly on the payroll, but they let me set up a table. I made decent money, too. But then the hotel staff thought I was taking away customers from their other services and they asked me to leave." Waiting for his reaction, she took another sip of water and asked, "Your thoughts?"

He seemed confused, but not scared like Kathy expected.

He smoothed out the cloth napkin on his lap. "Can't say I've ever heard that one before. It's interesting."

"Most people thought I was nuts. Especially since I didn't have a car, so I took the bus. To most of the city I was the crazy psychic lady. I'm surprised you've never heard of me." That was a lie. People on the bus definitely gave her quizzical looks, but she didn't have the reputation. At least, not to her knowledge.

"What was your niche? Tarot cards, palm readings, crystal balls?"

Kathy smiled. No one who didn't have at least a little knowledge about mediums ever asked about her niche. He was more interesting than she'd given him credit for. But there was still more left to tell—a lot more. If only he knew just how divine she was.

"I've never done tarot cards. I couldn't tell you how to read them. And if a psychic has a crystal ball at her table, run. She's a scammer. I mostly did palm readings. Occasionally, I did tea leaves as well, but the hotel didn't really like it when I brought in a dump bucket for the water."

"Could you read my palm?" He offered his hand, and she took it before she realized what she'd just agreed to. A lot of times she had an actual vision—an extension of her time specialty as a witch. She wondered if she would be able to see his future on command. Sometimes it was difficult to determine the difference between the reading and her feelings.

She forced herself to look down at his hand. Tracing some

of the wrinkles in his palm, she shared her findings. "Well, I see lots of stress...likely from your start-up. Conflict...passion...oh, but then here's success." She pointed a finger to a spot on his palm. "See that line? That's what's to come. This over here," she moved her finger, "that's what is."

"Can you see what was?" He looked up at her, and she realized they had been leaning closer to each other.

She sat back and reached for her water again. She opened her mouth to respond but was interrupted by the waitress bringing over the wine. Kathy breathed a sigh of relief. They were only twenty minutes into their first date and she was already searching his palms, hoping to see their futures connected. She needed to cool down.

"What do you think?" Will held up his wineglass.

Kathy took a sip and considered for a moment. It was rich. Full bodied with a hint of strawberry. She didn't know much about wine, but she knew this was good. "Very nice."

"It's only half as good as the food." He brought the glass to his lips but pulled it away before taking a sip. He raised it in front of him instead. "To a wonderful evening with a beautiful woman. How did I get so lucky?"

"Don't get too excited about that success in your future." She raised her glass and clinked it with his before taking another sip.

* * *

The Full Moon

After dinner, the two walked hand-in-hand to the end of the pier. The evening had gone perfectly. Kathy hadn't enjoyed a date so much in a while. She could already tell that things were different with Will.

The full moon was out, reflecting off Lake Erie and illuminating the sky. The glow from the city lights helped brighten the sky as well.

"It's beautiful," Kathy said. She rested her head against his arm.

"I like to come out here every so often just for the view. Presque Isle has an even better view, but—"

"I think this is perfect." She looked up at him and reached up on her toes to meet his lips. Kathy knew from his kiss that falling for him was a good thing—a great thing.

Prior to meeting Will, she'd felt completely burnt out from all the stress in her life: making a living with no skills an employer would be interested in, helping her sister raise Josh and Chris, and keeping up with her supernatural responsibilities was a bit too much at times. But standing out on the edge of the pier with Will completely erased all that, and for the first time in a long time, she was carelessly happy. All her subconscious thoughts were gone, and she was entirely in the moment.

The two were so consumed with each other that they didn't hear the splashing of the water. It wasn't until Kathy felt a slimy hand on her leg that her attention was brought back to reality.

She landed with a thud on the pier as something pulled her into the water. The water was up to her waist by the time Will had hold of both of her arms and pulled her up. The splash of the water hid the creature from sight, which Kathy was grateful for. She didn't want Will to see. She might be able to still pass this off as her being clumsy.

Once she was safely on deck, Will asked if she was all right. She barely had time to nod before Vepar lunged from the water and landed on the edge of the pier. He hissed at the couple, spraying them with water and slime.

Kathy put her hands up and froze both Vepar and Will. She needed to act quickly. She knew there would likely have been people in the hotel or farther down the pier who had seen or heard the commotion. She searched for her purse that held the potion to kill the water creature, but she couldn't find it. She must've dropped it in the water when he first pulled her in.

She needed to get Will away safely without exposing who she was. If that was even still possible. She could easily have unfrozen him and ran, but then she would be facing twenty questions about what happened. She wasn't ready for that conversation with him yet.

Before she could think of anything, her magic wore off and both Will and Vepar unfroze. The creature swiped at Will with his claws, tearing his blazer. Kathy pulled off her shoes and drove a heel into the creature's back. She saw the point of the knife she'd stabbed him with the week before and knew it

THE FULL MOON

wouldn't stop him. He turned and pushed her. Landing on the edge of the pier, she moved to get up, but when she shifted her weight she lost her balance and began to topple into the dark water. She gripped the bollard on the edge of the pier to keep herself from falling in.

Looking up at Will, she saw him charge Vepar, and a large sword appeared in his hands. Swinging it sideways, he tore through the creature's flesh and its head dropped to the dock. He kept swinging until pieces of Vepar scattered across the end of the pier. When he was done, he stood and admired his work, huffing and puffing. Kathy could see blood sprayed across his face in the moonlight. The sword in his hand disappeared, and he reached down to help lift Kathy back onto the dock.

He looked at her and said, "Grab the other end of the net over there and help me round up the body before anyone sees."

THANK YOU

This project would not have been possible without the support of my Kickstarter backers! Thank you all for your support!

Samantha Newberry
Sarah B.
Leslie Twitchell
Marlene Renteria
Rowan Stone
John Idlor
Erik S
Dead Fish Books
Troy Hill
Lou Paduano
Alexandra Corrsin
Daniel.D
Gary Phillips
Deborah Hedges

Thank you to the DN Publishing VIP Club members over at Patreon! Become a member and enjoy weekly perks!

Tracy O'Neil
Marguerite Goosby

patreon.com/DNPublishing

FIND ALL THE BOOKS IN THE COVEN SERIES!

More by the Author

To find more books by the author, visit
DavidNethBooks.com/Books

* * *

Subscribe to his newsletter to be the first to know of new releases and special deals!
DavidNethBooks.com/Newsletter

* * *

If you enjoyed the book, please consider leaving a review on Goodreads or the retailer you bought it from. Reviews help potential readers determine whether they'll enjoy a book, so any comments on what you thought of the story would be very helpful!

ABOUT THE AUTHOR

David Neth is the author of the Coven series, the Under the Moon series, Heat series, the Fuse series, and other stories. He lives in Batavia, NY, where he dreams of a successful publishing career and opening his own bookstore.

Also writes small town romance as D. Allen.

www.DavidNethBooks.com

www.facebook.com/DavidNethBooks